"Let's hope I have made amends for all the shocking humiliations I have heaped upon you, Sara," the earl said.

"That you can never do, my lord, except in a small way by removing your presence from Beechleys forthwith."

The earl was, she thought, a little taken aback at hearing such harsh words from such soft lips, as indeed he was, but he betrayed nothing of it. In a tone of exaggerated bewilderment he said, "Whatever have I done to merit such a scolding?"

"I wonder you dare ask."

"But I do ask."

Sara met his eye. "You can save all your pretty speeches for those who are gullible enough to enjoy receiving them," she said, closing her fan with a snap. "I know exactly why you are here, so do not think to gammon me."

THE THIEF
OF HEARTS

Rachelle Edwards

A FAWCETT CREST BOOK

Fawcett Books, Greenwich, Connecticut

THE THIEF OF HEARTS

THIS BOOK CONTAINS THE COMPLETE TEXT OF THE ORIGINAL HARDCOVER EDITION.

A Fawcett Crest Book reprinted by arrangement with Robert Hale & Company

ISBN: 0-449-23401-0

Printed in the United States of America

10 9 8 7 6 5 4 3 2 1

Chapter One

The post-chaise bumped and rattled along the rutted road, throwing its two passengers from side to side.

The elder of the two ladies in the face of this hardship clutched the strap in one hand and her vinaigrette in the other, saying in the faintest voice, "How I detest long journeys, Sara. They can transform the most robust person into the sickliest creature within a matter of days, and let no one say that I am in the least robust."

Her niece, sitting in apparent comfort, smiled. "It could be a longer journey, you know, Aunt, but take heart; we are nearly there."

"We shall not be at Beechleys until tomorrow afternoon, I collect, and all manner of nasty things could yet befall us." The chaise lurched over a particularly deep rut and Mrs. Carnforth gasped before sinking back into her seat, drawing a deep sigh as she did so. "It will be a miracle if we are not overset and crack our skulls. And if we do escape that fate the chances are that we will not escape Bill

Kersey, The Masked Fiend, or another of their rascally breed."

Her niece laughed. "Oh, I doubt if a highwayman will find us ripe for plucking, Aunt Phoebe. The Mail is, by far, more inviting."

Phoebe Carnforth made a faint noise. "We are not guarded like the Mail Coach, and you well know that if we are set upon the postillions will not come to our aid. What chance do helpless females stand at the mercy of a terrible rake such as Bill Kersey?" she demanded. " 'Tis more than valuables that he demands."

Sara laughed again, saying soothingly, "I'm sure we shall reach Beechleys safely. After all, we've been travelling for three days already, and none of the mishaps you've been foretelling since the outset have yet occurred."

Phoebe Carnforth made a faint noise again and the journey continued for a while in silence. Sara Auden, her hands tucked comfortably into a silk muff, occupied herself by gazing out at the passing countryside. She was fortunate to possess a stout constitution, which belied her slight build, and she never suffered from travel sickness. Whilst her aunt, with eyes closed, breathed laboriously at her side Sara's dark brown eyes took in the pastoral scene with interest. Her green redingote was not, perhaps, of the latest style but she certainly did not appear a dowd. With brown curls peeping out from beneath the brim of her bonnet, possessing a pleasant if not stunningly beautiful countenance, she looked some years younger than her five and twenty.

Some ten years previously, on the death of her vivacious and incomparable mother, Sara had emerged from the schoolroom to take over the running of her father's household, and never was it run so well. The late Fanny Auden possessed a slightly madcap nature, preferring to entertain her many friends and acquaintances, leaving the housekeeping to one who was paid to do so. Needless to say during Lady Auden's lifetime Beechleys had been well run but never excellently—not until Sara took the task upon herself.

Sara had an elder brother, Farley, who was heir to the estate, and a younger brother, William, who had been no more than a baby at his mother's death. There were also two younger girls, Margaret and Angelina. Sara had supervised their upbringing with all the diligence and affection of a mother and in the past ten years had earned for herself the reputation amongst her relatives for being sensible and extremely reliable in times of trouble.

This being undoubtedly so, on the demise of her uncle, Hubert Carnforth, the Vicar of Somerton in the county of Derbyshire, she had been immediately dispatched to bear the widow company in her bereavement, a duty, it was considered, that Sara was well suited to fulfil. Sara had expected to stay with her aunt for only a short while, intending to escort her back to Beechleys. But Aunt Phoebe, hard on the death of her husband, contracted bronchial pneumonia which almost put an end to her life. Her recovery, fortunately, had been sure, if slow, and when she was strong enough to travel she had borne her niece to Harrogate to spend the autumn and winter at that, now unfashionable, watering place in order to recover her health and spirits.

Now, at long last, Sara was going home and no manner of discomfort during the journey could dampen her excitement at the prospect. Incredibly almost a year had passed since she had seen her brothers and sisters, and Sara especially longed to see Margaret who had been married to the squire's eldest son for some three years and was the proud parent of a little girl, with another child soon expected. Sara had not seen her little niece since the child had been little more than a babe in swaddling clothes and Margaret had recently written to say that Wilhemina was now walking with only the aid of leading strings.

"I wish you hadn't persuaded me to travel by post chaise," Aunt Phoebe complained some time later. "I cannot help but feel my own carriage, shabby as it is, must be more comfortable."

"That is undoubtedly so," Sara agreed, going on to point out, "but we discussed the matter thoroughly and you know full well that going by carriage would have made a far slower journey and we would have had to send our trunks by carrier. As it

is the carriage should already have reached Beechleys and all our clothes pressed and hung."

"I hope you may be right. I just cannot rid myself of the feeling that our clothes might now be lying in a ditch, or even adorning the hussy of some
footpad."

"Oh, Aunt Phoebe!" Sara cried, more out of
amusement than vexation, "you're far too much of
a pessimist. If I'd had my way," she added with a
gurgling little laugh, "we should have travelled by
Mail. It's a wonderful way to travel, so I'm told.
Such style and dash, and no stopping at the toll-
gate."

"How can you talk of travelling with the riff and
raff, Sara? Even so, having that horn blown in my
ears each time a toll-gate was approached, would
make me quite ill with the headache. The dangers
of being overset must be far greater than even in
these rattly contraptions. There's always some
young buck to tip the coachman to hand over the
ribbons."

"Well, just think! Before long we shall be home.
The summer is always good at Beechleys and when
the Season begins you'll be going to London for
Angelina's coming out. There's so much to look
forward to."

Angelina was Sara's youngest sister and undoubtedly the beauty of the family, the only one except-
ing the elder boy, Farley, of all the Auden children
who resembled their dead mother. Sara, her sister

Margaret and the young William favoured their less spectacular father.

Phoebe Carnforth brightened at her niece's words. "I must own that is certainly something to look forward to. It's more years than I care to recall since I participated in a London Season, Sara. Not that I regret marrying poor Hubert," she hastened to add. "He was a very handsome man in his prime, even though he was only one year off forty when we were married. I never had cause to regret a moment of our married life, my dear. I only hope you may be as happily settled before long."

Sara smiled tightly at hearing such oft spoken words once more and turned to stare out of the window. "I should not rely on that, Aunt," she murmured. "Never having received an offer of marriage in the past I am not likely to receive one now."

"If that is so, Sara, I feel it only right to tell you that it is only because you don't encourage likely suitors. I don't say you should throw yourself at a man's head; that would be quite improper. But you could give a little encouragement."

"Aunt Phoebe, I have never met a man I've wanted to encourage in the least, let alone throw myself at his head. You'll find it far more satisfying to concentrate on seeing Angelina suitably fixed."

"That I most certainly will do, although if your sister fulfils her earlier promise of beauty there will be little enough for *me* to do. But depend on it I shall also try to make a match for my favourite niece. There must be many a man who would welcome a wife with your experience of housekeeping, apart from your other—not inconsiderable—accomplishments. The trouble is that you freeze them off."

When Sara looked at her aunt all amusement had gone from her countenance. "Like the odious Mr. Stacey with his seven motherless children . . . ?"

Phoebe Carnforth shifted in her seat, unable to meet Sara's frank gaze. "There are other men who are respectably placed. You have good looks, Sara, and a fine figure, but let me speak plain; at five and twenty you don't have to be too choosy."

"I am only choosy in as much as wanting to marry for love, Aunt Phoebe. If the opportunity doesn't come along then I shall stay on the shelf and not regret it."

Mrs. Carnforth gasped. "Don't let me hear you utter such nonsense again, Sara. You'll not remain a spinster, not while I am still able to draw breath. It's only a pity you didn't have a Season. You would have been easily fixed, I don't doubt."

Sara smiled again. "If Mama had lived nothing would have prevented my coming out, but someone had to look after Papa and the children as you well know. And to be truthful, Aunt Phoebe, it's as well. Meg and I would have hated a Season. Angelina, now, was meant to enter Polite Society. She'll be

the rage of the ton. And remember, Aunt, Meg
didn't need a Season to secure a husband."

Mrs. Carnforth heaved a deep sigh and Sarah
saw with consternation that her skin had taken on a
greenish tinge. "Too true. I suppose it was fortunate that Meg and John only had eyes for each
other all their lives, even if it is an unexceptional
match. They're happy."

"So they are," Sara agreed.

"I can't wait to see little Wilhemina. Will they be
at Beechleys do you think?"

"I hope so, if Meg is up to it. She tires so easily
these days, which isn't so surprising."

"I've no worries about her happiness, and Farley
will find himself a bride before long, I've no doubt.
He always had a good sense of duty. He must realize that your father isn't getting any younger."

"He's not in his dotage yet, Aunt Phoebe, so
don't let Papa hear you speak of him as if he were.
And the last time I spoke to Farley his talk was all
of horses, certainly not females."

"But that's quite natural, child. Your father was
just the same until he clapped eyes on Fanny." She
smiled at the recollection, adding, "Of course Angelina will make a brilliant match. I've no worries
on that score either."

On which score the good lady did worry needed
no mention. Both ladies knew what it was. Like
most married ladies Phoebe Carnforth regarded
spinsterhood with the greatest distaste. From what

Sara understood of the matter Aunt Phoebe, reaching the end of her second Season with no better offer forthcoming, had been so afraid of being left on the shelf that she had accepted Hubert Carnforth's offer with alacrity, even though his living was only modest and his private means small. But being old enough to remember her parents' happy marriage and seeing how happy Margaret was with John, Sara wanted nothing of a loveless match for appearances sake, whatever were Aunt Phoebe's sentiments on the subject.

"The thought of it quite takes me back," Aunt Phoebe reminisced. "Not that it will be strange to me; I've kept abreast of all the on-dits all these years. I know just who to invite to our little soirées, never you fear. Dear Lady Gurney, my dearest friend, has kept me well informed through her frequent letters." She clutched at her vinaigrette again and closed her eyes. "Oh dear, I do feel unwell."

Sara leaned forward anxiously. "We must stop the chaise, Aunt Phoebe, so that you can take the air."

"No, no. We mustn't stop—not here in open country. A highwayman may be in the area. Nasty man. Shocking rake. I heard tell of one young woman on the Birmingham stage." Her voice was all but a whisper as she recounted the shocking tale. "He took a fancy to the poor creature. Abducted her and not one of her fellow travellers raised a finger to stop him."

"If he was armed that's not so surprising. They wouldn't dare to try and stop him."

"He kept her a prisoner for three days—and nights." This was barely audible.

Sara held the smelling salts beneath her aunt's nose and if the terrible tale related by Mrs. Carnforth struck even the tiniest spark of terror into her heart she betrayed none of it. Instead she said in a light tone, "If it happened to me people would say I was fortunate to attract the attentions of even so base a creature, having no one else in view."

Mrs. Carnforth groaned, but whether this was due to such unseemly words being uttered by her niece or to her own sickness was not quite clear. Without further hesitation Sara directed the postillions to stop, which they did but only after swerving perilously to make way for the Mail Coach, as it was always given preference on the highway. The thundering hooves of the Mail Coach team flew past and melted into the distance in a remarkably quick time leaving in Sara's mind a picture of the armed guard at the back and the windswept and mufflered outside passengers in front.

The moment the chaise jolted to a standstill Sara lost no time in leading her aunt outside, and it was not a moment too soon. "There," Sara said soothingly a moment later, "you do feel better now, don't you?"

Her aunt merely nodded as she lifted a lace-edged handkerchief to her lips. At the sound of hooves on the road nearby Mrs. Carnforth stiffened, saying, "Oh dear, I do hope no one has seen."

"No, I'm sure not. It can only be a passing farmer. We're well hidden behind this thicket, never you fear."

"Thank heavens I shall have the summer at Beechleys in which to recuperate from this ordeal. I'm sure this journey will yet be the death of me, my dear."

"Nonsense, Aunt," Sara answered briskly. "I cannot allow that. You must certainly live long enough to see our little Wilhemina—and, of course, the new baby."

Mrs. Carnforth allowed herself a laugh. The colour was returning to her cheeks, much to Sara's relief. "I hope I may live to see *your* children, Sara."

Sara's eyes glittered with a strange brilliance. "If you are feeling better, Aunt, I think we should continue on our way. We have stayed here long enough."

Aunt Phoebe, being nearer to the road, led the way out of the thicket. Almost immediately she gave a loud shriek and as Sara emerged to clutch at her aunt's trembling arm her eyes alighted on a terrible sight.

The postillions were cringing against the chaise whilst a man, astride a grey cob, masked and enveloped in a dark blue riding coat, pointed a pistol in their direction.

At the sight of the two ladies the robber smiled, doffed his beaver with his free hand, and said in a deceptively mild voice, "Good afternoon, ladies. Bill Kersey at your service."

Sara, fearful that Aunt Phoebe would dissolve into hysterics at any moment found that her own fear was fading fast. "We have no valuables, sir," she said, staring him in the eye, which was not an easy feat as she was small and he was tall, made to look even more daunting above her astride his horse. And there was a disconcerting light in his dark eyes; a look of mischief, more than malice, which put her in mind of the awful tale Aunt Phoebe had told, making her blush under his bold stare.

"Our belongings and small amount of valuables were dispatched by carriage four days ago, sir. We only have a small amount of money to see my aunt and myself to our destination. We are not ladies of means."

His dark eyes did not waver from hers. "One so fair of face as you, ma'am, cannot be considered without means." He quickly doffed his hat again. "Now, please, without further delay be so good as to give me your reticules. You too, ma'am." He motioned to the older woman who shrank, wide-eyed and unusually speechless, against the side of the chaise. She shook her head at which the highwayman said, "Come now, ma'am, you would not wish me to make you."

"Please, Aunt Phoebe," Sara begged, "do as he says, I beg you."

Phoebe Carnforth began to weep into her handkerchief and Sara was beginning to lose patience with her. If they gave this man what little money they possessed they could be on their way unmolested in a matter of minutes.

"Your niece is a sensible girl, ma'am, as well as being quite beautiful. You would do well to heed her words." He hesitated a moment and Sara hoped he did not notice the flush that was creeping up her cheeks. Sara was not used to blushing, but neither was she used to being called beautiful. "You may have heard that I held up the York Stage a week ago," he informed the weeping widow. "On it was one young lady who pleaded that she had no money or jewellery. I found it hard to believe and subsequently found several pieces of fine jewellery concealed about her person."

Aunt Phoebe gave a shriek and the postillions began to titter, albeit nervously, until Sara shot them a fierce look. Mrs. Carnforth was sobbing harder and made no attempt to stop her niece from removing her reticule and handing it, together with her own, to the robber.

"I beg you to let us go on our way now. My aunt is of a nervous disposition and has recently been ill."

"You plead very eloquently, ma'am," he said taking the reticules. He held them by their strings for a moment or two, never taking his eyes from Sara's face and she was well aware that he was debating with himself a question. What that question may be she tried not to think upon. She was, however, unable to hold that brilliant gaze any longer and stood with eyes downcast.

"Oh, do come away!" Aunt Phoebe pleaded as Sara bravely stood her ground, uncomfortably close to the highwayman.

A moment later, without even glancing inside them, the robber handed back the reticules into Sara's hand. She looked up at him then in surprise but before she had a chance to speak he said, "A lady of such loyalty and breeding must needs be telling the truth. I'll not deprive you of your last guineas. 'Tis wild country in which to be abroad with no money."

Sara felt no relief of tension. Her throat was tight and her mouth dry, and she felt terror well up inside her breast as he leaned over to lift her hand to his lips. At that moment she feared that he would demand payment of another kind. She drew her hand away quickly as Aunt Phoebe cried, "Oh please leave my niece be. She is a good girl; a comfort to all her family." But Sara was unable to draw her eyes away from his.

Her aunt's words, spoken sincerely, gave her no comfort. Suddenly she saw herself as she really was; worthy of saving for being a comfort to her family rather than a woman with hopes and dreams like any other.

"Have no fear, ma'am," Bold Bill replied. "I happen to have taken a fancy to your niece, but unfortunately I cannot stay to make her acquaintance, so for now you may continue your journey untroubled." He returned his attention to Sara. "Your name, ma'am?"

"Sara Auden," she answered, her voice no more than a whisper.

"And where are you bound, Miss Auden?"

"My home. Beechleys, Dome End, Hertfordshire."

The highwayman sat back in the saddle and Sara found her heart beating unusually fast. He took the reins in one hand and doffed the beaver again. "Perchance we'll meet again, Miss Auden."

With that he headed back to the road, leaving Sara experiencing strange emotions which were soon banished as she hastened to attend her half-fainting and hysterical aunt.

Chapter Two

It was late the following afternoon that the post chaise bowled up the avenue of Beechleys. The terrifying experience of the previous afternoon still figured largely in the minds of both ladies—although for different reasons.

They had put up, the previous night, at an inn not far from the scene of the crime, and on hearing the dreadful story the landlord's wife had immediately borne Mrs. Carnforth to her bedchamber in order to administer hartshorn and water, thus leaving Sara free to ponder on her meeting with Bold Bill Kersey—the scourge of the highway.

As she listened without commenting whilst her aunt recalled the event, somehow she could not feel he was such a rogue. He had not taken their money and apart from affording them a nasty fright had done them no harm.

He had spoken, not like a common rogue, but with the tongue of a gentleman, and there had been a hint of laughter in the eyes of the man who was accredited with some dreadful crimes. It was as if his chosen way of life was more of an adventure rather than a necessity born of poverty, for he had not been shabbily dressed either. Sara could not easily dismiss the way he had looked upon her, the kiss he had bestowed upon her hand, nor the fact that he had called her beautiful. Even though aware that the tongue of a man such as he could not be trusted she could not forget he had spoken such words.

Inside her unawakened emotions were fighting their way to freedom and Sara was glad when at last her aunt had her summoned to join her.

By the morning Mrs. Carnforth had recovered from her ordeal to such an extent that she partook of a particularly hearty breakfast. For the remainder of the journey to Beechleys she chattered non-stop and therefore did not notice that her niece was for once somewhat subdued. However, Sara's spirits soon rose again at the sight of familiar landmarks and her joy knew no bounds as the chaise turned in at the gateway. After a short ride along a beech-lined avenue the mansion, of modest proportions, became visible to the travellers. It was situated on a slight rise with green lawns starting almost at the door and rolling as far as the eye could see. There were larger houses and far more handsome ones but to Sara it was home and never had she been more glad to see it.

When the travellers were handed down from the chaise several servants were waiting at the door to greet them, together with an excited Angelina.

William was at present at school and Farley at pursuits that were befitting a fashionable young man of means.

Angelina, with fair hair and wide blue eyes, was indeed a beauty. Wearing a gown of palest blue cambric she no longer looked the child Sara had left behind less than a year before.

The sisters hugged each other joyfully and then held each other at arm's length. "How you've grown, Angy!" Sara exclaimed at last.

"Wait until you see how William has grown, Sara. He's going to be taller than Farley, which reminds me; Farley has written to say he'll be down next week, and imagine! He's bringing some of his set with him." Sara stared at her sister in amazement. "Oh yes, he is. I was never more surprised in my life. He suggests we have some kind of an entertainment and Papa has agreed that we are to have a party. With musicians for dancing too!"

"This sounds quite unlike our brother," Sara said with a laugh.

"Oh, he's quite changed, Sara, you may be sure. He's in a much smarter set now and his clothes are far more fashionable too. His appearance wouldn't shame Mr. Brummell himself. Our brother has become a bang up blade and no mistake."

Sara laughed even more. "Amazing! It sounds as if a female might be the cause."

Angelina's blue eyes betrayed surprise. "Oh, I never thought of that, Sara. But it still doesn't answer why he's bringing his cronies to Beechleys. Nowhere could be duller, especially after London. Still," she added thoughtfully, "perhaps Society is a little thin at the end of the Season." She smiled and dimpled prettily. "I don't much care why, Sara; we will enjoy the benefit. It will give me the chance to practise my waltz before my come-out. Oh, it is good to see you again, Sara! Mrs. Jameson is the kindest soul but nothing ever runs smoothly when you are gone. And you know how my hemming leaves much to be desired. It was never so good as yours."

Mrs. Carnforth just then bustled over to her nieces and hurried them into the hall. "Stop this twittering, you two. I must go to my room immediately. Mrs. Jameson has warmed the bed and is bringing up some wine. Our trunks have arrived safely, Sara, which is more than can be said of *us*. I'm quite fatigued." She peered at her youngest niece. "Your sister and I have had the most dreadful experience . . ."

Some days previous to her arrival at Beechleys Sara's elder brother received a letter from his sister informing him of her imminent departure from Harrogate. Like most young men of his time, possessing a sizeable income, his life was spent in the pursuit of pleasure, his main concern being that his clothes were not up to the latest fashion. Despite his preoccupation with himself, his horses and his pleasures, Farley Auden had the odd distinction of being fond of his family, especially his sister, Sara, who had kept his home comfortable after the death of his mother. But the letter he received caused him some qualms and even when, later in the day, he went to Brooks's to keep an appointment with a friend a frown was still upon his face.

He was so deep in thought that his dearest friend, the elegant Lieutenant Matthews, had to address him twice before attracting his attention.

"Oh, hello, Matty," said Farley with little enthusiasm as he looked up at his friend with a pair of blue eyes remarkably like those of his youngest sister. With fair curly hair cut short in the current style he was a remarkably handsome man, and as the heir to a baronet and the possessor of a respectable fortune he was much sought after by the young ladies of the ton.

Young Lieutenant Matthews seated himself next to his friend. "Something the matter, Farley?"

"Nothing important."

"Not been losing at hazard, eh? Tricky game hazard, although I must say I have a liking for it myself."

Farley shook his head. "I'm not that much of a fool, Matty. When the luck's against me I throw in my hand."

"Hm. Then it must be *la belle Francaise* who's cast you in the dismals. Don't bother to deny it.

Can't say I've ever met a female who put me in such a frame of mind."

Farley laughed. "No, it's not that either. She hasn't given me reason to believe she likes me better than anyone else but she hasn't snubbed me either as she did to Booker last week. And she did make a point of telling me the date her parents were removing to Brighton at the end of the month. I'll be going too of course. I'll have to declare myself soon or I'll lose her for certain." The thought steeped him even further into gloom. "Although now I come to think of it Genevieve is something to do with it. It's my sister really."

Lieutenant Matthews laughed. "Do stop talking in riddles, Farley. Has your sister met Genevieve then? Have they taken a dislike to each other?"

Farley let out a hoot of laughter at the very idea. "Dislike Genevieve! Impossible. I tell you Sara would love Genevieve."

"Then what is troubling you?"

"I can rely on your discretion, Matty?"

"Don't you know it?"

"If I tell you what's teasing me you can tell me I'm a fool and that'll be an end to it. If Genevieve agrees to marry me I must be the luckiest man alive, but that in itself presents a problem you see. It means she will be mistress of Beechleys and what will Sara do then?" His friend looked at him blankly.

"What most other females do in such a position, I imagine."

"That's what troubles me. I've never thought of it until recently. You see, Sal has looked after us and run Beechleys for ten years. It means everything to her. If only she would get married *first* she'd have her own home, d'you see?"

"Yes, I do," his friend admitted. "It's a pity you're so fond of your sister. Myself, I wouldn't care."

"Well, it's there and that's how I feel."

"Is there no chance of a match?"

Farley shrugged. "She's halfway to thirty," he explained, "and she meets only bumpkins. Meg married John Plant, who in truth is a dull dog but a worthy fellow. She's perfectly happy but it won't do for Sal, and when I bring home a bride, which I hope to do before long, Matty, Sal will be no more than a maiden aunt with no real home of her own, and that won't do either—not for Sara.

"If I thought she'd come up next Season I'd be happier but if I know Sal she'll stay at Beechleys and leave the social scene to Angelina and my Aunt Phoebe."

"Hag faced is she?"

"Good Lord no!" Farley exclaimed. "Angelina is the beauty of the family but Sara is certainly a handsome woman. Yes, certainly she is. She should have had a Season, you know. Would have had offers by the score, but my mother died and there was an end to it. No one to bring her out, and besides she wouldn't have stood for it with us all at home and William still in the cradle. Strong sense of duty has Sara. Too strong now I come to think of it. We've all relied on her too much. Selfish beasts, family."

"Well," considered his friend a moment later, feeling slightly uncomfortable, "I'm sure the matter will settle itself. You see if it doesn't."

"Dammit, it won't!"

"Hasn't your sister any chance of meeting a prospective husband?"

"It's not likely now."

"Then," said Lieutenant Matthews brightly, "you'll have to invite a few likely matches to Beechleys. There's no other way to do it."

Farley Auden stared at his friend as if he had taken leave of his senses and Lieutenant Matthews added quickly, "Invite only those you know want a wife and in no particular need of a great fortune. Nobby Lostwith is one. He's been hanging out for a wife for three seasons to my sure knowledge. His father refuses to part with one single guinea more until he's fixed with a wife."

Sir Henry Auden's heir stroked his chin thoughtfully. "No one would come, Matty. Everyone has their own estates and dislike visiting. They only do it out of necessity or duty. Why should they come to mine while the Season's still on and Brighton's only a month away? With no hunting to speak of there's little enough to do."

"It's only for a few days mind," Matty pointed out. "You can rely on me to make up your numbers, needless to say. You might get a few takers, Farley. The end of the Season is almost upon us; appetites getting jaded and all that. Shooting and fishing might look inviting. Just the right time. James Lastley lost a fair packet at hazard the other night; he might be glad of a few days out of town. Try Melford too. I heard him say he was going down to Melford Park and that's near to your pile." Lieutenant Matthews sat up straight in his chair, excitement gripping him. "Melford's just the one. Right age too, Farley. You'd do well to settle him with your sister. Melford has a title anyone would be glad to have in the family. Make a push to invite him. He's your best chance, rely on that."

Mr. Auden was still thoughtful. "Yes, I can just see Sara as a countess. Yes, I fancy that. I wouldn't like to see Lastley as my brother-in-law though. He always gambles too deep for my liking, and I don't believe Nobby would settle for my sister's portion. It's genteel enough but far from considerable. Melford, now, is as rich as Croesus and a good judge of horseflesh too." Farley Auden frowned suddenly, "But *he* won't come. He's still tied up with that bit of Covent Garden company at the moment, and she's costing him a packet too by all accounts. Still can't help liking the fellow. The shine on his boots matches that of the Beau himself. Wonder what'll become of Brummell now. That's a rum business. Besides Sal isn't Melford's type. He always likes the flashy kind I've noticed." He looked at his friend. "But you might have a good idea there, Matty. In any event it can't do any harm. I've got to go down to Beechleys to pay respects to my aunt so I may as well take some company too."

He got to his feet and smoothed a small wrinkle from his skin tight pantaloons. "Let's have a stroll, Matty, and see if we can find any likely contenders for the hand of my sister."

He offered Lieutenant Matthews his arm and as they sauntered out, pleased with their plan, they were unaware of the young man sitting directly behind them, shielded from view by a colonnade. As the two young men went out of the club the silent listener folded his newspaper, which to all intents and purposes he had been reading. The man stared after the other two. He frowned slightly for a moment before suddenly smiling to himself and following them out of the club.

Dinner was served much later than usual the evening that Sara and her aunt arrived at Beechleys. Later still, after tea was served in the small drawing room and Sir Henry was ensconced in his study with the estate accounts and his customary bottle of brandy, the three women eagerly chattered with scarcely a pause for breath. (One of the reasons why Sir Henry had excused himself from the tea ritual that evening.)

Sara was already busily stitching, completing the sampler she had started whilst still in Harrogate. Angelina sat beside her sister on the brocaded sofa and twirled a blonde curl around one finger.

"I helped Betsy to unpack your trunks, Sara," she said after a moment's deep thought.

Sara looked up from her sampler and smiled. "That was very good of you, dear."

"I do recall," her sister continued in much the same tone of thoughtfulness, "you seem to have several new gowns; all of them in the latest style."

Aunt Phoebe peered at her youngest niece. "Sara was badly in need of new clothes and I had no intention of being seen in the company of a dowd. I heard tell of an excellent seamstress in the Spa and commissioned her to rig out your sister. It was little enough thanks for the selfless way she nursed me through my illness. My physician told me my recovery was due in no small amount to Sara."

Having said her piece Mrs. Carnforth sat back whilst Sara said nothing; she simply coloured a little. Angelina's pretty mouth drooped slightly. "I'm sure *I'm* the one to know Sara's worth, Aunt. Didn't she nurse us all through our childish ailments?" She looked at Sara again, her eyes widening ingenuously. "But I had *no* idea Harrogate was such a fashionable place these days."

"You must know very well that it isn't," her aunt

retorted sharply, "but we did receive all the latest magazines and had the styles made up accordingly."

"You must have attended many assemblies, Sara," her sister probed.

Sara looked up sharply, frowning as she did so. "How could we whilst Aunt Phoebe was in black?"

Angelina's blue eyes opened even wider. "Forgive me. I forgot. It was the white satin dress that made me think of it. The one with the blue overdress of net." She laughed lightly. "You will make me look quite a dowd next week when Farley comes with his ton friends."

Sara didn't even look up from her embroidery. "That we cannot allow. By all means wear the dress yourself. I shall wear another."

"Oh, I couldn't."

Aunt Phoebe was about to say something of the kind too only Sara silenced her with a look, saying easily, "I was never happy with it. Beautiful and fashionable as it is it never did suit me. It's the shade of blue I think. With only a small alteration it should fit you perfectly."

Aunt Phoebe frowned and Angelina said with little hesitation, "Well, if you're sure, only I have no shoes to match."

"Naturally I have those too," her sister answered, "and if I am not to wear the dress I have no need of the shoes either. You may have them also. The blue overdress is precisely the colour of your eyes, Angelina. I thought so when we chose the material. It's a shade that always makes my eyes appear dull. I don't think I would have worn it in any event."

"I have tears in two petticoats," Angelina complained a moment later as she watched her sister neatly stitching, "and my stitchery just isn't neat enough, Sara."

Her sister smiled. "You must let me have them tomorrow. I'll have them repaired in a trice."

"Oh, I knew you would! You are so good, Sara."

"She was absolutely marvellous when that rogue held us up," their aunt commented looking up from her own embroidery. "She stared him straight in the eye. She didn't beg. Oh, no. She just spoke to him rationally, which is more than he deserved let me tell you. What a scoundrel! Daring to kiss Sara's hand! But she kept her head. Oh, yes. I must say Sara is wonderful when trouble strikes. There's not another like her, I'll be bound."

Sara kept her eyes on her embroidery, not daring to look at either her aunt or her sister for fear that they would be aware of the strange emotions she experienced whenever she was forced to think of that encounter. There was something about his eyes that had affected her oddly and try as she would she could not dismiss the memory from her mind.

During the previous night she had lain awake for hours, allowing her imagination to wander, to imagine what it might have been like to be cast up behind Bill Kersey and to be carried away with him. She spent a good deal of those wakeful hours scolding herself for being affected in such a way. She blamed her fixation on the number of novels she had been forced to read as a release from the deadly boredom of life in Harrogate. She vowed then never to read another and in the future only to think thoughts seemly for a woman of her age and breeding. But, good as her intentions were, she could not stop her mind from wandering back time and time again to the way a certain scoundrel had looked upon her and set her heart racing.

She became suddenly aware of Angelina's eyes upon her and as she glanced at her sister the girl said, "Poor Sara. Was it such a dreadful experience?"

"Not really. It might have been worse," Sara answered in a level voice. "He took nothing from us."

"Praise be to the Lord for that," her aunt interpolated. "You were in my care. If anything . . . *anything*," she repeated with a shudder, "had happened to you I don't know how I would have faced my brother."

Sara put down her sampler, thinking that, perhaps, if her aunt were not so garrulous on the subject she, herself, might be able to put it from her mind. "You mustn't allow it to upset your nerves, Aunt. It is over. Quite finished. We will never meet him again." At her own words Sara could not help but feel despondent.

"It is to be hoped so," Mrs. Carnforth muttered,

"although I cannot feel it finished until that rogue swings from the end of a rope."

It was Sara's turn to shudder. She knew she was wrong but she could hardly bear the thought of the brilliant light in those dark, burning eyes, being extinguished for ever.

"Sara always keeps her head. I remember once, quite clearly, when William choked on a fish bone Sara was the only one rational enough to turn him up." Angelina lay a hand on her sister's. "You were very brave but I cannot believe you were not very frightened, my love."

"And I cannot believe he was so alarming," Sara answered in a strangled voice. "He acted quite the gentleman, there's no doubt of it."

"I should have been terrified," Angelina admitted. "I should have swooned away; died of heart failure even."

"I almost did," Phoebe Carnforth cut in, not to be outdone. "If he had kept us a moment longer I'm persuaded I should have fainted right away."

Angelina looked at her sister again, her worried countenance giving way to a smile. "They say he's quite handsome."

"He was masked," Sara answered slowly, "and he had a muffler up to his chin. But I'm quite sure beneath it all he is quite a handsome man."

"Oh, how could you tell?" Aunt Phoebe demanded. "You were in no mood to notice."

Sara smiled sweetly and pointed out, "You were swooning, Aunt, not I."

"I was not in such a taking that I didn't see how huge and menacing he was."

"Well," Angelina said to her aunt's annoyance, "seeing no great harm was done to either of you it was a great adventure and one I wish I could recount when I go up to London next Season. I'm sure it would take me out of the commonplace." Then with an air of appeasement she turned to her aunt. "I've been practising my pianoforte, Aunt Phoebe, and I'm much improved. Would you like to hear me play . . . ?"

Chapter Three

It was almost a week later that Farley Auden bowled up the avenue in his curricle and pair. Sara, who had been on the look-out for him, rushed to the door and stared in amazement at the elegant young man who stepped down.

The last time she had seen her elder brother he had been attired in the most bizarre style, sporting such language that she could hardly make sense of anything he said. Today as he removed his riding coat adorned with several capes she could see that his mode of dress had undergone a drastic, but welcome, change. His coat was of the soberest hue and his waistcoat was adorned with only one fob. On the previous occasion his loudly-patterned waistcoat had been adorned with several large seals and fobs and his shirt collar had been so high and so stiffly starched he could barely move his head.

Her immediate reaction was one of dismay. It seemed that in her absence Farley had grown up. He was no longer an aspiring dandy with no thoughts other than his clothes and his horses; he was now an accomplished man-about-town.

Farley handed his high crowned beaver, his gloves and his whip to Maitland, the butler, and, turning to Sara, grasped her hand. "Welcome home, Sal. It's good to see you. Father has never stopped complaining that nothing is to his liking when you are away."

Sara laughed and squeezed his hands. "Oh, it's good to be back, Farley! And good to see you too. You really are what Angelina calls a bang up blade!"

Farley threw back his head and laughed. Without any further consideration for his coat or his neck-tie he pulled her close and hugged her tightly.. When he let her go at last she said, "Looking as you do it's a wonder the Society mamas will let you out of their sight. You must be one of the most sought after young bucks in London."

"Naturally," he answered with a laugh and then, lowering his voice; "As a matter of fact, though, only one girl takes my fancy."

Sara looked at him eagerly. "Oh, do tell me, Farley."

He hesitated a moment and then said, "You're not to tell anyone. This is for your ears only, Sal. She's already had two offers to my sure knowledge so there's no certainty . . ."

Sara danced up and down with impatience. "Do tell me, Farley. I promise I won't say a word, although I dare say she'll jump at your offer. Her other beaux cannot be as handsome as you."

"Her name is Genevieve L'Estallier. Her parents fled from the Terror but she was born in England. I hope you may like her, Sal."

"I shall love her if you do," she answered, puzzled by the troubled look in his eyes. It could not be the uncertainty over Mademoiselle L'Estallier's affections, as the mention of that lady had put a great shine on his countenance only moments before.

"I've not made an offer for her yet," he pointed out a moment later, "and I'm not the only runner in the race."

"I refuse to believe that, Farley." She pulled away from him. "I must change this dusty old gown before dinner so you must excuse me, dearest. Papa will be back soon."

"Where is the old girl?" he asked, adopting a fashionably languid air.

"If you mean Aunt Phoebe, she has been complaining of the house being upside down these past few days, which it has of course. As you know Angelina insisted upon having a rout for your guests so invitations have had to be issued, linen aired, rooms turned out and so on. I cannot recall having so much glassware and plate out at once, but," she added truthfully, "I've enjoyed myself as much as Angelina has enjoyed the planning of it. Mrs. Jameson's an excellent housekeeper . . ."

"But not as good as you," her brother interpolated.

"There were matters needing my attention," she amended with a dimpled smile, "and the talk of the party has certainly diverted everyone's attention from Bold Bill Kersey." She saw the question in his eyes and quickly added, "I'll tell you of it another time. As to your previous question, Angelina has taken Aunt Phoebe over to the Manor to visit Margaret."

"How is Meg?" he asked.

"Blooming," she answered.

"You've seen her then?"

"Several times since we came back. Marriage and motherhood suits her so well, and Wilhemina is so sweet. It's quite delightful having a baby around again."

Farley watched his sister cross the hall. His thoughts were still troubled, but anxious as he was to see Sara set up in her own establishment he couldn't imagine why he had fallen in with Matty's mad scheme, for mad it certainly was.

After their conversation Farley had accosted several of his friends, but had only received acceptance of his invitation from four of them apart from Lieutenant Matthews. As Beechleys was in no way a great mansion it was as many London guests as they could accommodate, but on reflection Farley realized that Robert Booker, the Honourable Tom Cheviot—heir to Viscount Dawley—and Desmond Adams were certainly as unsuited to Sara as the Prince Regent himself. Matty, of course, could be counted out. At present he was wedded to his horses and only came along to lend support to his friend during his enforced rustication.

Which left only Lord Melford. This gentleman was troubling Farley a great deal. His Lordship couldn't exactly be called a good friend of his, being several years older, but it seemed fated that the earl should have accosted him on entering Watier's later that same evening, and in the course of the ensuing conversation informed young Auden that he was about to spend several days at his country home and found it boring in the extreme.

"You must stay with us," Farley had blurted out without a further thought after receiving an encouraging nudge from his friend. "My sisters are having a rout. Nothing like the ton parties of course," he hastened to warn him, "but diverting when one is obliged to rusticate."

Lord Melford appeared to consider for a moment and Farley bitterly regretted his hastily uttered invitation. "I'd be delighted to accept your invitation," the earl had said after a while. "I can't think why we haven't visited before. I collect that our estates are only twelve miles apart. What could be more convenient?"

He bowed stiffly and after informing his still reluctant host that he would be arriving on the day of the party he took his leave.

Farley was still puzzled and the worst of it was that Melford was not Sara's type either. He had a preference for beauties and fond of Sara as he was Farley was fully aware that his sister's looks fell far short of beauty.

For some odd reason of his own Melford wanted to be included in the party and Farley had the gravest misgivings. He cursed Lieutenant Matthews silently for thinking up such a loose scheme. In all events Melford would probably take a fancy to Angelina the moment he clapped eyes upon her and amuse himself by indulging in a flirtation with the chit. That was the last thing Farley wanted to achieve. Angelina was pretty enough to find a gallant for herself and was already full enough of her own consequence without Melford's attentions adding to it.

However, Farley's uncomfortable thoughts were immediately thrust from his mind on hearing the sound of carriage wheels and many horses' hooves coming to a halt outside his front door. Sara was already at the top of the stairway and as two loudly dressed young men came laughing into the hall, followed a moment later by a third, she leaned over the baluster rail to see the three newcomers apparently congratulating her brother on some score. It took only a second or two for Sara to realize, wryly, that the four friends had chosen to relieve the boredom of the journey in typical fashion by treating it as a race.

Rather an unequal race, Sara thought as she went into her room. Farley, apart from being an excellent whip, had the advantage of knowing every bend and rut in the road.

Sara smiled to herself, happy to be home. She had enjoyed the past week enormously, having endured lodgings in Harrogate for several months past. Now everything at Beechleys was spick and span as she liked it, and it was going to be good seeing the house alive with activity, as it used to be when her beautiful mother was alive. Seeing Farley again had relieved her mind of a nagging worry. She had hardly been aware of it until now. In the past she had feared that he was a little too fond of whist and horse-betting, but now, it seemed, he had grown out of that phase with no ill coming of it, and no doubt it was due to a great extent to his affection for Mademoiselle L'Estallier.

Sara was even more delighted at the prospect of her brother bringing home a bride even if it did mean handing over management of her beloved Beechleys to that lady. Sara had always known, and indeed hoped, that the day would come, yet as she glanced around her she knew there would be a great void in her life when she was obliged to make her permanent home in the Dower House. Even William, now that he was at Eton, could no longer be regarded as a child who was in need of her ministrations. Involuntarily her eyes misted as she stared out of her window across at the rolling lawns that fronted the house. The thought, at that moment, of Bold Bill Kersey was an involuntary one and she felt suddenly warm despite the chill in the air.

Dinner was a gay meal with Farley and his friends filling the large dining room to a great extent.

"One cannot help but shudder at the thought of what those young bucks get up to in London," Aunt Phoebe whispered to Sara later that evening, "but I must own that their manners have been exemplary tonight."

Angelina, as was to be expected, bloomed in the company of so many gallants in her own home (yet another buck had arrived hard on the heels of the other three) and needless to note the visitors, despite being undoubted connoisseurs of beauty, responded to Angelina's naïve charm in a manner as warm as the girl herself could have wished.

"I'm convinced our coming rout must be the most successful ever held in the county," Angelina exclaimed when the ladies had adjourned to the large drawing room, leaving the men to their port. She was wearing a dress of buttercup yellow muslin with long sleeves and the fashionably high waistline and low neckline, which had caused Aunt Phoebe to frown when she had first set eyes on it. But Aunt Phoebe was the first to admit that the dress did become Angelina who was, in her aunt's shrewd opinion, likely to become the rage of the ton.

"I hope you may be right," her sister commented.

"I must own to be looking forward to it. With Farley home and Margaret bringing Wilhemina for a stay tomorrow, it's going to be the happiest time we've had for years."

"But think how dull it will be *afterwards*," Angelina said in sudden dismay.

"Not for long," Aunt Phoebe pointed out. "You must prepare yourself for the Season and that will occupy you well, for you are far from being as accomplished as I would wish."

Angelina, ignoring her aunt's mild stricture, clasped her hands together. "That will be marvellous. Lieutenant Matthews—only fancy, his regiment is the Regent's own, the tenth Hussars—has been regaling me with such witty anecdotes I feel as though I know so many people already. He said he will certainly stand up with me for the waltz at Almacks."

Aunt Phoebe looked scandalized. "He will do nothing so improper!"

"Oh, the waltz is quite respectable these days," Angelina answered with a languid air. "Only rustics still think it improper." Sara quickly stifled the laughter that was bubbling up inside her as Angelina went on heedlessly, "Mr. Cheviot says I must ride with him in the Park in his phaeton. He has a team of chestnuts for his phaeton and a pair of greys for his curricle. And he knows everyone, absolutely everyone who is anyone in Society. He'll be Viscount Dawley one day, you know."

Phoebe Carnforth scowled across her embroidery. "I know Dawley and a stupider man I never met. I hope, miss, you don't intend setting your cap at a *Viscount*'s heir. I intend better things for you."

Sara grinned and Angelina began to giggle behind her fan. "Oh, Aunt Phoebe, really. I just find him amusing."

Just then the doors to the drawing room were thrown open and the men were ushered in. Aunt Phoebe laid aside her sewing, saying with a benign smile, "Perhaps you would sing for us, Angelina, while Sara accompanies you on the pianoforte."

Blushing in the correct manner Angelina protested that her voice was nowhere near good enough for such discerning company, whereupon a chorus of male voices insisted that one with so fair a face must also possess the voice of a lark . . .

Later that evening after Sir Henry had retired, slightly bewildered at the influx of young males into his household, his sister set forth to seek him out. She had left her nieces happily poring over fashion magazines whilst the men sat down to a rubber of whist.

Mrs. Carnforth found her brother in the library and when she entered he looked up, a scowl marring what was quite a handsome countenance. "Noise, noise, noise, there's no escape from it," he complained and added pointedly, "I'm not even free in here."

Mrs. Carnforth ignored his inhospitality and settled her not inconsiderable weight into a chair. "I don't know what you might expect when the house is filled with young people. For myself I admit, after Harrogate, I don't object to it."

"Young people. More likely a pack of strutting peacocks."

Phoebe Carnforth laughed. "I can easily recall Papa wearing much more colourful rig, Henry, and as for noise it was, by far, more noisy when dear Fanny was alive. Never a week passed by without a houseful of guests and a party of some kind."

"I was younger then."

Phoebe Carnforth was not put out. "You should be delighted. It will keep you ever young, Henry. I only wish poor Hubert and I had been blessed with children. It was our greatest disappointment, you know."

Her brother gravely nodded his sympathetic agreement, adding by way of comfort. "At least you don't have to put up with this infernal noise."

She wagged a finger at him. "Now don't pretend you're not glad I've brought Sara back to Beechleys."

Sir Henry's face brightened. "I won't quarrel with that statement, Phoebe. D'you know? Nothing goes right when Sara's away. It's quite amazing. Not enough starch in my neck-cloths for one thing—or too much, and more likely than not Maitland will bring up the wrong claret or the mutton's overdone. Can't abide overdone mutton and never could. It never happens when Sara's here. Sensible girl, my Sara. More sensible than the others put together."

Phoebe Carnforth stared at her brother thoughtfully for a moment or two before saying, "That's the trouble with her," and when her brother looked up she added, "Too sensible—or so people think."

"Why are you talking in riddles, Phoebe? Is there something wrong with m'daughter?"

"Only in as much as she's not married."

Sir Henry sank back into his chair. "She's never wanted to be."

"She's never had the chance," his sister amended.

Sir Henry avoided Mrs. Carnforth's searching gaze. "She's not a hopeless case yet. Plenty of men would be glad of a girl like Sara for a wife."

"Precisely, but there aren't many men Sara would settle for, I can tell you that. She was approached several times while we were in Harrogate, but she never gave one of them cause to hope. She was civil as always, but beyond that . . ." Aunt Phoebe ended with a shrug of dismay and then added, "None of them were exceptional men but respectable certainly. You mark my words, Henry, one day Sara is going to fall for someone quite unsuitable and have her heart broken. It's always the way with females who are considered 'sensible'."

Sir Henry stared down at his desk top for several moments before saying in a ponderous voice, "That being the case I don't think there is much we can do to prevent such a calamity occurring."

"Oh, you're quite unfeeling, Henry. I am quite out of patience with you. Is that what you want for your daughter? A daughter who has been as good as Sara, who deserves so much more?"

"Come now, Phoebe, this is only supposition. It may never happen. In fact I'm sure it never will. In any event Sara is a spirited girl and used to having her own way. There's nothing anyone can do to stop her having her way, although should she become enamoured of this unsuitable fellow I'm persuaded she will behave with the utmost circumspection as always." He smiled smugly. "Sara will do nothing to bring shame on to the Auden name. We're her world, you know. She cares for no other."

"And whose fault might that be?" his sister demanded.

Sir Henry's eyes shifted again. "Can't help poor Fanny dying. Three physicians couldn't save her; no expense spared. Someone had to take over the house. If Fanny had lived Sara and Margaret would have been brought out and in fine style, as you well know. Aye, and I'd probably have been forced to mortgage my estate to do it. And a waste of time and money it would have been too! Can you see Sara and Meg simpering and curtseying in London drawing rooms? Meg's a good girl too. No nonsense about her either."

"You're a fool, Henry Auden, let me tell you. Sara's made of a different stuff to Meg. There's more of Fanny in Sara than any of you know and if you think Sara would settle for a dull dog like John Plant then you're more than a fool, you're a raving idiot!"

Sir Henry shifted uncomfortably in his chair. It had always been his fate to be ruled by women; in his youth by this same awesome sister, during his marriage by his lovely Fanny, and afterwards to a certain extent by his eldest daughter.

"There'll always be a place for her here," Sir Henry went on doggedly. "I don't know what the fuss is about suddenly."

"Well said," applauded his sister. "The fact remains that like the rest of the family you've taken what Sara's had to give selfishly. I'd be happy enough to have Sara with me to keep *me* company for what little time I have left on this earth, but what of afterwards, when we've gone? Sara's fate you know very well. She'll divide herself between her sisters' and brothers' establishments, playing with their children, nursing invalids and knitting for the poor. And the trouble is, Henry, there's nothing we can do about it. I can introduce her to several men but Sara would have no one of an arranged match. She wants to marry for love!"

"The girl's been reading too many contemporary

novels," diagnosed her father. "It will have to stop."

"You married for love, and although few would believe it, so did I, which puts me in mind of what I really intended to speak of; I shall need some money." At the mention of such a precious commodity her brother looked up sharply. "Now don't look at me like that, Henry. Angelina will need a whole new wardrobe before we go to London, not to mention her Court dress. It is essential, you realize, that she should be presented."

"Good grief! My family are out to ruin me!"

"Nonsense. You escaped bringing the two elder girls out. You owe it to Fanny's memory to do what is right by Angelina in fine style. No less will do."

Sir Henry groaned. "You'd better let me know how much you will need, but bear it in mind that I am not a rich man."

Phoebe Carnforth smiled. "You've been singing that same sad tune for as long as I care to recall, Henry."

"Sara's done nothing but beg the blunt all week for this dratted party tomorrow. It will cost me a small fortune in champagne and candles alone, apart from the food and the hire of the musicians. Now there's an extravagance. In my day young people were obliged to make their own amusements."

"You have a short memory, Henry. Besides, since Fanny died you've not entertained at all and ten years is a long time to wear black. Everyone is going to have a good time and it's excellent preparation for Angelina."

"But so much champagne. And we surely don't need *every* chandelier alight. The chandler's bill makes painful reading already."

Mrs. Carnforth, brushing aside Sir Henry's complaints, went on heedlessly, "I notice Farley is becoming a most presentable young man. The sight of him makes me feel quite my age although I'm glad to see he no longer aspires to the dandy set. I can't fault his dress now, not loud like it used to be. He looks quite the gentleman. You mark my words, Henry, you can thank a female for *that* . . ."

Chapter Four

A million lights twinkled from the great chandeliers in the small ballroom which had been built on to Beechleys when Fanny Auden became its mistress almost thirty years before. The house had been raided for its best furniture and this was now arranged around the perimeter of the dance floor for the comfort of those unable or unwilling to dance. Almost a hundred invitations had been issued to the most important families in the county and, as most of the older members recalled Fanny Auden's extravagant routs, a great majority of the replies had been acceptances.

Sara gazed around with pleasure. Everyone seemed to be enjoying themselves, some making new acquaintances and others renewing old. Dressed in a simple gown of figured velvet with puff sleeves, and a coronet of flowers in her hair, Sara presented a trim figure. She floated in and out of the crowds, too good a hostess to consider her own enjoyment above the comfort of her guests. Not that she had been obliged to forgo her own pleasure; she had already stood up for two country dances, one with her brother-in-law John, and the other with the vicar's son—a gentleman about to take Holy Orders himself. He was two or three years Sara's junior, but this consideration had not dampened the ardour he had felt for her for many years, and consequently, as in the past, Sara spent much of her time avoiding his unwelcome attentions.

Farley Auden fingered his quizzing glass before yawning discreetly behind his hand. He wondered when he could decently spirit away his friends to a side room for a rubber of whist. His eyes caught those of a matron wearing a confusion of feathers in her enormous turban and he bestowed a stiff bow and a quick smile upon the lady, which caused her to turn away in a fluster of embarrassment.

Farley was even more irritated with himself than he had been on his arrival. He longed to be back in London, although his friends, to give them their due credit, did not appear unduly bored. But, then, unlike himself, none of them were longing for sight of Genevieve L'Estallier.

It was a dreadful mistake, he believed, to have considered influencing Sara's life by inviting a selection of unsuitable young men to meet her. With every minute that passed they looked more unsuitable and Farley felt more and more foolish at ever having embarked upon such a scheme. In the future he vowed to let life take its natural course and until he was, himself, married, only to visit his filial home when the occasion warranted. Compared to the fashionable routs to which he was now accustomed the entertainment and company tonight was decidedly rustic, and, having been persuaded to invite guests down, he would now be obliged to remain much longer than the necessary night or two.

He lifted his quizzing glass in the languid way adopted by the man of mode and surveyed the scene through it. He stopped abruptly as his gaze came to rest upon a blushing damsel who had apparently taken a fancy to the handsome young heir to Beechleys. As the girl lowered her eyes, her blush deepening considerably, Farley Auden allowed his glass to fall and sighing with resignation went to engage her for the next set.

Sara came back into the ballroom after a considerable absence, having remained in the supper room to make a last minute inspection of the table, which almost groaned under its load. As she cast an experienced eye over the various dishes presented for her guests' delectation she made a rapid calculation and reckoned that there would be enough to satisfy even the heartiest of appetites.

The moment she came out of the supper room she saw Aunt Phoebe bearing down on her from across the room. Aunt Phoebe looked quite daunting under her large turban of turquoise satin which was adorned with a profusion of matching feathers that floated around in the air as she moved.

"Our little party is going to be quite a success,"

she said, bowing to a new acquaintance across the room. "I cannot recall when I've enjoyed myself more."

She plumped herself on to a small sofa and, glad of a moment's respite, Sara sat down next to her, fanning herself furiously. "Angelina is having a wonderful time. I do believe she has been engaged for every dance so far."

She looked across to where her sister was now partnering Lieutenant Matthews and not for the first time did she notice his partiality for Angelina. But this was only to be expected. Angelina, clad in the white satin and blue net gown, was by far the most fetching female in the room and was being eyed with some disfavour by other girls less well endowed.

"That is only to be expected," Aunt Phoebe said echoing Sara's thoughts, her keen eyes darting about in an effort to miss nothing. "How often have you been engaged to dance, may I ask?"

"Several times," Sara answered quite truthfully with a laugh. "Only it was mostly by men with whom I would not wish to stand up! Lieutenant Matthews is quite amusing though; Angelina didn't exaggerate on that point, Aunt. He's quite a delightful young man."

"Humph. I don't doubt it. A man in the Regent's regiment must needs have pretty manners. So long as Angelina keeps herself sufficiently aloof and gives no encouragement all will be well. With her

looks she should snare a duke no less. A marquis at
the very least!"

Sara's ready laugh erupted again as the music
ended and she was engaged for the minuet by Farley. "You could show a little more enthusiasm," she
scolded as they danced.

"Sorry, Sal, but there's a girl by the name of Mil-
licent Drew who's taken a fancy to me. Can't escape her, and I'm dashed if I can stand a girl with
buck teeth."

"Oh, Farley, you're too cruel! She's not at all an
ill-looking girl. It's simply that you have eyes only
for Mademoiselle L'Estallier—admit it."

He smiled. "Too true, Sal. I wish I were certain
of her affections though. Still, I know a pretty girl
when I see one and it's a sad day when a fellow's
sisters are the handsomest girls in the room."

When the music ended Farley, thankfully, went
to quench his thirst on some of the excellent champagne Sir Henry had been forced to supply for his
guests. Sara stood at the edge of the dance floor,
smiling as she caught the eye of a dowager who,
from the way she coloured up, was obviously discussing the Auden family with the elderly man in
her company.

Another country dance was about to begin and
Sara felt relief when she realized that the evening
was well and truly under way and Angelina had not
yet secured her father's permission for the waltz to
be played. Sara was certain the sophisticates in the

metropolis no longer found the new dance outrageously sinful, but there was no doubt that by far the greater portion of the guests present tonight would be scandalized at the sight of it.

She smiled encouragingly at Aunt Phoebe who was being led on to the floor by John Plant's father, an incongruous sight as the squire was as spare a figure as Phoebe Carnforth was large. Sara fanned herself furiously; it was growing exceedingly hot in the room but she was sure a suggestion of opening a window would only be met with dismay. She drew out a dainty lace-edged handkerchief which was soaked in eau de cologne and pressed it to her cheek, feeling cooler immediately. During her sojourn in Harrogate Sara had whiled away the time by embroidering and edging enough handkerchiefs to last the entire family some years.

As the music struck up her eyes alighted on Angelina. Tonight there was no doubt of that young lady's popularity. In her gown of white and blue, with her huge blue eyes peeping out from beneath a crown of wispy curls done up in a coronet of pearls, she looked quite as angelic as her name suggested. Sara's gaze transferred itself to her sister's partner as together they made a most striking pair. Angelina's partner was as dark as she was fair and he was quite the tallest man on the floor, Angelina's head hardly reaching the shoulder of his dark blue evening coat.

Sara's interest quickened as she stared at him.

She couldn't place him although his bearing was not unfamiliar. The excellence of his evening clothes, the short curly hair, proclaimed him immediately as one of Farley's London friends, yet he had not been amongst those who had arrived yesterday.

When, a moment later, he was turned in her direction a tremor of recognition shot through her body. It couldn't be! She closed her eyes for a fraction and when she looked at him again he was saying something to Angelina which immediately caused the girl to laugh, and her laugh, like the music, echoed and bounced around in Sara's brain.

Any moment now the man would sense her stare, yet she could no more stop looking at him than scream just then. *"Perchance we'll meet again . . ."* he had said. But she had never dreamed that he would have the effrontery to come into her home. She felt a flush spread up her cheeks. She had readily given him her name and address when she could have, just as easily, refused to identify herself. But, then, she had never really believed it was anything other than a few carelessly uttered words from a renowned womaniser—or had she? She was certainly aware that the scoundrel had hardly been out of her thoughts for a week.

The dance ended and, rousing herself at last, she went to seek out Aunt Phoebe. Sara's chin came up stubbornly. A notorious highwayman had somehow gained entry to her home, but this time he had been too bold; there were more than enough able-bodied men present to make sure of his capture. The rogue would be in jail before the night was over, of that Sara was determined.

Aunt Phoebe, bosom heaving, plumped down in a gilded armchair and, feeling that her legs might not support her a moment longer, Sara sank down next to her. As Aunt Phoebe fanned herself furiously Sara sought out the felon with her eye. He was now in the midst of a group comprising Farley, Lieutenant Matthews, her brother-in-law, John, and Angelina, who, in a way that struck even more fury into Sara's breast, was looking up at the newcomer and laughing at whatever witticism he happened to utter.

Sara leaned over and plucked at her aunt's arm. "Aunt Phoebe," she said in a low voice, not taking her eyes off the handsome stranger, "do you see that man over there? The one who is standing next to Farley."

How dare he come to Beechleys and pass himself off as a gentleman!

"John, dear?" asked Aunt Phoebe, peering across the room.

"No, on the other side of Farley!" When Phoebe Carnforth's eyes came to rest upon the stranger's imposing figure her face took on an expression of stark disbelief. Sara sank back into the chair. "You recognize him?"

"My dear child, of course I recognize him. I'd

know him anywhere." She put one hand over her breast. "My goodness! Oh dear, oh dear. It gave me quite a turn to see him there. Like a ghost. Quite like a ghost."

"Well, what are we to do? He must be brought to justice, only I don't want to spoil the party while it's going so splendidly, yet we mustn't allow him to escape."

Aunt Phoebe at last drew her eyes away from the attractive group and looked at her niece. "What are you talking about, child?"

"Bill Kersey. How dare he come here and spoil our party! I daresay he heard speak of it and thought it a good opportunity to give us a fright so soon after the hold-up."

For a moment Phoebe Carnforth said nothing, and then with an air of total bewilderment and mounting excitement, "Where is Bill Kersey? Here? *Here?*"

"Aunt Phoebe, you've just recognized him!"

"Recognized whom?"

Sara, for the first time in her life, wanted to scream and kick, and in general strike out. The rogue could escape at any time and here was Aunt Phoebe acting obtuse in the extreme. "Bill Kersey," she managed to say.

Phoebe Carnforth began to fan herself even more furiously and as an afterthought began to fan her niece instead. Sara pushed it away irritably. "I insist that you drink no more champagne tonight," the widow said, her lips settling into a tight line of disapproval. "I do believe you are fuddled, Sara."

"I've only had one glass of lemonade, Aunt, and you *did* recognize him."

Aunt Phoebe closed her fan with a snap. "If you've drunk no champagne I can only assume that you have a fever. Of course I recognized that young man. He couldn't be anyone other than one of Harry Merrick's cubs. I knew Harry before I met your dear uncle." She smiled suddenly and rather foolishly. "All the girls set their caps at Harry, and it wasn't because of his title or his fortune either. He married Ariadne Bethington. She was a handsome girl, still is I daresay. She was extremely stupid though and I daresay she's still like that too. If my calculations are right that's the eldest boy, Richard. I've heard that he is as wicked a flirt as his father was before him. Had all the hopefuls in despair for Seasons.

"He paid great attention to Lady Gurney's Sylvia for a whole Season. She told me that in one of her very interesting letters. Of course it meant nothing but Lady Gurney is convinced it caused Captain Pershore to make Sylvia an offer, and of course they're very happily settled." Mrs. Carnforth gazed at him thoughtfully for a moment or two. "I expect now that he's inherited the earldom the pressure's on for a match. He'll be about thirty or a little more I should think, so it stands to sense he'll settle before long."

Sara, famed for her level-headedness, was fast becoming more and more bewildered and did indeed begin to wonder if she were raving. "An earldom," she echoed in a faint voice.

"That is what I said," snapped Aunt Phoebe. "Bill Kersey indeed. You're having a belated reaction to that episode as I knew you would."

Sara rallied slightly. "No, no, Aunt Phoebe. It isn't that at all. I tell you that man is the highwayman who held up our chaise. I recognized him the moment I set eyes on him this evening."

"And I tell you that if you persist in making an accusation of that sort you will end up in Bedlam. That is the Earl of Melford. It can be no other. He is the very double of his father at the same age. Bill Kersey indeed! Whatever will you say next I wonder. Bonaparte's masquerading as the Duke of Cumberland no doubt! Just look at him, Sara. Does he look like a highwayman?"

Out of the corner of her eye Sara could see that he was now speaking with Margaret who, owing to her condition, was merely a spectator of the evening's events. Rage flared within Sara again at the sight of the smile on her sister's face.

"He would hardly appear in his driving coat and mask," Sara retorted, scarcely able to conceal her anger.

"I don't want to hear you make such a ludicrous suggestion again," Phoebe Carnforth said. "You wouldn't recognize that rogue again if he stood before you."

"I would," Sara insisted, recalling every detail of his face, such as she'd been able to see.

"The rogue was masked and mufflered. You're talking utter nonsense." As if to emphasize her desire to end the distasteful discourse Phoebe Carnforth then turned to the lady on her right hand and began to engage the spinster in earnest conversation, leaving her niece near to tears.

Sara felt she just could not explain why she would know the highwayman again. Aunt Phoebe would be outraged if she did so. But Sara was frustrated at her aunt's failure to recognize him as Bill Kersey. Without another witness who was able to identify him there was no chance of bringing him to justice, although she was well aware that time usually took care of such matters. Highwaymen rarely lived to enjoy old age and the spoils of their trade, and the knowledge, for the first time, gave her outraged sensibilities some comfort.

Unwillingly Sara's eyes were drawn to him again. Now, after apparently procuring a glass of lemonade for her sister, he looked completely at ease sitting next to Margaret and employing her in earnest conversation.

Sara's eyes took in every detail of his clothes, his black knee-breeches, the white waistcoat and exquisitely cut coat, the broad shoulders of which owed nothing to padding unlike, she suspected, the coats of several of the men present. Even the lace on his shirt was of the finest quality. The fact that he was so elegantly attired with enough address to pass himself off as a gentleman did nothing to soothe the rage in Sara's breast, instead it heaped fuel on to the fire.

It was only a moment later when she realized she had been staring at the supposed Earl of Melford for some time, for now His Lordship himself was staring back. His dark eyes were filled with mocking amusement as they came to rest upon her face. And as Sara met them levelly she felt that same stab of excitement run through her veins. Almost immediately she lowered her eyes and concealed her flaming cheeks behind her fan, and a moment later when Lieutenant Matthews came to claim her hand for a cotillion she was glad to stand up with him.

As she danced her feet performed the steps automatically; her mind was so far away that Lieutenant Matthews had to speak to her several times before he elicited a response. On two occasions the stranger passed close to her, having Angelina for his partner once more, but he made no sign of having noticed or recognized Sara. Seeing him at close quarters did nothing to allay her fears regarding his secondary identity. True, as Aunt Phoebe had said, he had been muffled and masked, but Sara felt that she would know him anywhere, and did. And at the time of the hold-up had she not noticed par-

ticularly that the highwayman spoke like a gentleman and not at all like a common robber, whom
she was given to understand often used the foulest
language even in the company of ladies?

Sara frowned at him as he passed, but he was
deep in conversation with Angelina and apparently
insensible to all else. Aunt Phoebe had identified
him as the Earl of Melford and Sara knew that
despite thirty years in the Parish of Somerton Mrs.
Carnforth, due to her dear friend Lady Gurney,
had been able to keep abreast of all Society news
during that period. The more Sara considered the
matter the more she realized that this man, so elegantly attired with such a manner of address and a
friend of her brother, must indeed be Lord
Melford, which presented another problem for her;
why should a peer of the realm pose as a highwayman? Almost immediately the question she had
posed herself answered itself. He would not. He *was*
Bill Kersey as well as being the Earl of Melford. A
tremor of terror shot through her, making her miss
her step. She shot an apologetic smile at her partner, knowing that she was possibly the only person
alive who was aware that Bill Kersey and the Earl
of Melford were one and the same man.

Having partially recovered from the shock of this
realization Sara began to wonder why he had been
led to commit highway robbery at all. The obvious
answer would be a pressing need for funds, but
Sara knew that if a wealthy man was suddenly in

such dire need of money her aunt would certainly know of it. Anyway, such a need was usually ascribed to gambling debts and no amount of hold-ups would provide enough to repay them.

As the cotillion came to an end Sara was forced to the reluctant conclusion that Richard Merrick had resorted to highway robbery for what the young bucks of the ton called a lark. She had heard of the outrageous pranks perpetrated by these bloods simply to relieve their boredom, or for the want of something new to do. She had always harboured a secret fear that Farley may be among them. If he was, or ever had been, Sara was glad that no news of it had reached her ears. Becoming a highwayman, however, might just be the daring lark to appeal to an active young man with a great fortune, able in the sporting arts, and a success with any woman with whom he cared to flirt. He could use his position to shield him from suspicion. Sara, at the thought of such injustice, became incensed anew.

It was somehow forgivable for a man who was in despair, living in dire poverty and the sordid sur-roundings Sara believed existed, to try and escape them in such a way, but for a man to do so merely for the fun of it was despicable. It was a great mis-take to assume that only ill-bred ruffians plundered the High Toby. Sara recalled the story of the noto-rious highwayman, James Maclean, who had lodg-ings in fashionable St. James Street and enjoyed *affaires* with many of the Society beauties of his day.

With a guilty start she realized that Lieutenant Matthews was addressing her yet again. "I do beg your pardon," she said, bestowing a conciliatory smile upon him.

"It was of no importance, Miss Auden. I was just remarking on how lively your party is. Most enjoyable."

"It's kind of you to say so, Lieutenant Matthews, but it must be exceedingly dull compared to ton parties."

"By no means, I find new company most refreshing." He considered her for a moment. "You seem rather preoccupied, Miss Auden. I do hope such an influx of guests hasn't been too wearing on you."

She smiled. "I'm quite used to keeping house, Lieutenant Matthews, and it's a very welcome change to be surrounded by so many people. You may not be aware of it but I have spent the autumn and winter in Harrogate with my aunt, and to be charitable Harrogate is not the liveliest of places in which to be."

"I have spent only one night there," he answered, his eyes twinkling, "and one night was sufficient I assure you, although I saw enough of the Spa to enable me to appreciate your preference for company now, however."

The earl passed close by them and Sara spoke, in order to keep the conversation flowing so that the lieutenant should not think her churlish. However provoking was the earl's presence Sara knew she must not lose sight of her first duty to her guests. "My preoccupation," she replied, "was due to the presence of someone I didn't expect to see tonight."

The lieutenant's eyebrows went up a fraction. "I trust no one has upset you, Miss Auden."

"No, no," she said quickly as the dance ended, much to her relief. No good would come of confessing her suspicions of one of her guests. To her chagrin she realized that the robber would probably leave Beechleys free, having fulfilled his promise to meet her again. The vanity of the man almost overcame her.

Lieutenant Matthews escorted her back to where Aunt Phoebe was sitting and bowed briefly to both ladies before hurrying off, Sara didn't doubt, to engage the more loquacious Angelina for the next set. Sets were being made up for a quadrille and as Sara fanned herself she saw that the vicar's son was approaching her. He was rather a red-faced young man, his complexion having taken on an even ruddier hue than usual after his several efforts on the dance floor.

"My dance, I think," he said when he came up to her. He smiled at her with a confidence that irritated.

Sara forced a smile to her face and was about to accept his proffered arm when an authoritative voice said, "You are mistaken, sir. I believe I had engaged Miss Auden for this set myself."

Before she summoned up enough courage to look at the intruder Sara knew who it must be. She shot him a furious look from behind her fan and met his amused gaze.

Charles Hanley's face grew even redder at this interruption. He pulled indignantly at his waistcoat. "I beg *your* pardon, sir, but Miss Auden is engaged to stand up with me."

The newcomer displayed no such excitement in his bearing. He was calm as he fixed the unfortunate man with a steely stare, saying in a pleasantly cold voice, "I must inform you, sir, that I am addressed as my lord, not sir," adding in a quelling tone, "Are you refuting my word?"

Charles Hanley with none of his lordship's manner or physical presence, and certainly none of the social graces of the ton, detested such frippery people and was a passionate believer in his rights. He was about to voice further protestations at the usurper when Sara said quickly, "His lordship is right, Mr. Hanley, I'm afraid I quite forgot that I had promised this set to him."

Charles Hanley, the possessor of an excellent memory, looked incredulous. Sara was furious at being forced to lie, but she knew full well that Charles Hanley was no match for the Earl of Melford, either verbally or physically, and she had had a horrific vision of the earl calling the inoffensive man out. And that was something Sara wasn't prepared to have on her conscience despite her revulsion at the prospect of dancing with the rogue.

Charles Hanley fell back, murmuring something unintelligible, and Sara was forced to accept the earl's proffered arm. "Miss Auden," he said as if the foregoing exchange had not occurred, "allow me to introduce myself . . ."

"I already know who you are," she answered in a carefully controlled voice, whilst physically shaking with anger at the man's audacity towards her for yet the second time in as many weeks.

He checked slightly in surprise before continuing to lead her on to the floor. "I am honoured, ma'am," he said, bowing slightly. "I hope you'll accept my apologies for my late arrival. Family matters detained me longer than I had expected."

Still seething, Sara only managed to nod as the music struck up. For a few minutes she concentrated on her steps in an effort to blot out his disturbing presence from her consciousness.

"Why do you frown so?" he asked at last. "It was not such a crime, you know."

His voice was filled with amusement. How she hated him his ability to mock her so mercilessly while she had no hope of serving him in kind. "It was unforgiveable," she murmured. She flashed him a dark look. "Mr. Hanley is no match for such as you, and you know it. You took unfair advantage of his mild nature and his inexperience."

"He allowed me to," the earl replied with honesty.

"How unfortunate for you," she scoffed. "I'm sure you would have liked him to challenge you. I think it would give you great pleasure to kill an innocent such as he."

"Certainly not! I abhor bloodshed and I would hate to take up a challenge from one who would obviously be an unequal shot."

She recalled that Bill Kersey had never yet killed a man, although there was nothing to indicate that he never would. "I wish I were a man, Lord Melford," she said, her eyes blazing at him. "I would call you out and I assure you I would not be an unequal shot."

His lips curled into a smile. "If you were a man the trouble would never have arisen. Neither myself nor any other man in the room would desire you as a dancing partner. But I must thank Providence for designing you a woman. I don't believe I would be a match for you if you were not. However, I fail to believe that you would rather have that excuse for a man as your partner."

Sara felt her cheeks redden. "I would rather have *any* man in this room as a partner."

His eyebrows rose slightly at such vehemence but his good humour did not desert him. "There was never anything in your brother's attitude to indicate he possessed a shrew for a sister, therefore I refuse to believe that you are. It's good to see such spirit in a woman, especially one who cares so deeply for her fellow human beings, which I believe the gentleman can lay claim to be despite being clad in the oddest style."

"Mr. Hanley is a man who has more important matters to attend rather than his clothes."

Lord Melford looked deliberately bewildered and as he replied, "Is there anything of greater importance?" she knew he was mocking her again.

Her chin came up determinedly. "It is strange, I find, that my brother has never before numbered you amongst his acquaintances, my lord."

He didn't answer immediately and when he did it was in a thoughtful way. "Let us say we have known each other for some considerable time, and when he was good enough to invite me to your lovely home when he heard I was to be in the area I was delighted to accept."

His lips twitched as he attempted to prevent himself laughing out loud. Sara did not miss the gesture and felt that he must be enjoying himself hugely at her expense. The music ended and Sara could hardly believe that her ordeal was over at last. She could only hope that he had gratified his humour and would now leave her alone. Without a further word she sketched a curtsey and made to move to the edge of the dance floor, only an importuning hand prevented her.

"I cannot let you go until you grant me your forgiveness, Miss Auden."

She swung round to face him again, her eyes searching his face questioningly. For a moment she had the mad desire to beg him, implore him, to give up his thieving ways, but could not find the courage to do so.

"Forgive you?" she said in no more than a whisper.

His smile reached his eyes. "I cannot help but feel you are still angry on behalf of that red-faced youth who is so unworthy of your favour."

She stiffened. "Your apologies are due to Mr. Hanley, my lord, not I."

"Then I will offer them to him."

"Which will, you must recall, make me appear a liar, for I told an untruth to save him from your wrath."

He smiled again. "In that event I will have to hold my tongue. A few kind words from you, however, or even a mere smile in his direction will be sufficient to soothe his wounded pride and restore his good humour, I fancy."

The musicians were preparing to play again and Sara and her partner were still on the dance floor. When a waltz was announced a gasp of dismay rippled around the assembled company.

Lieutenant Matthews and Angelina were foremost on the dance floor and as the music began Sara angrily started across the floor. She had gone but a few steps when a strong arm encircled her waist and a voice close to her ear said, "This dance is mine also."

"Pray let me free, my lord," she gasped as he whirled her away.

"You cannot pretend you are engaged elsewhere for _this_, Miss Auden."

"I cannot perform the steps, my lord. Please let me free."

More young couples were following the example of those already on the floor despite the disapproving stares of many of their elders. As Sara passed him she noticed to her amazement that her father was smiling and tapping his foot in time to the music.

"The waltz is quite acceptable, Miss Auden," her partner assured her, "even by Royalty now."

It seemed an interminable time before she was released from his iron grip. "I shall never be able to face my neighbours again," she fumed, hiding her burning face behind her fan.

"Nonsense. You could hardly refuse to do a dance performed at your own rout, Miss Auden. They will recover from their momentary outrage by tomorrow and talk of this evening with awe for years to come. Only see how your sister has enjoyed it."

"It isn't seemly," was all she could manage to murmur in her confusion.

He gazed at her for a moment, a look of concern replacing the one of irony. "You are in need of refreshment, I feel. Allow me to escort you to the supper room."

There seemed no point in further argument. He would have his way regardless, she was sure. He was a man who brooked no argument, and she was in need of a glass of lemonade.

The Earl of Melford escorted Sara into the quieter supper room where the air was fresher, and as he did so she was not so lost in her frustration that she did not notice the envious glances she was attracting from several young ladies of her acquaintance.

He was absent from her side for only moments before he returned to where she was sitting on a sofa in an airy alcove. He handed her the welcome glass of lemonade, his eyes never leaving her face and his presence disturbingly near.

"Let's hope I have made amends for all the shocking humiliations I have heaped upon you, Miss Auden," he said after a few moments.

Glad of the short respite Sara had regained both her breath and her wits. "That you can never do, my lord, except in a small way by removing your presence from Beechleys forthwith."

The earl was, she thought, a little taken aback at hearing such harsh words from such soft lips, as indeed he was, but he betrayed nothing of it. In a tone of exaggerated bewilderment he said, "Miss Auden, whatever have I done to merit such a scolding?" adding with acidity, "not to mention such a breach of good manners."

Sara flushed slightly again at censure which, if she were honest with herself, she fully deserved. However she regarded such rudeness as justified on this one occasion, knowing he also must be only too aware of how justified it was.

"I wonder you dare ask."

"But I do ask."

She gave him her empty glass which he disposed of together with his own. When he looked at her again she was able to meet his eye. "You can save all your pretty speeches for those who are gullible enough to enjoy receiving them," she said closing her fan with a snap. "I know exactly why you are here so do not think to gammon me."

To her satisfaction his complaisance faded. He looked surprised and, yes, she was sure, angry. "Do you indeed?" he said softly.

Feeling more relaxed now that she had caused him some small measure of discomposure Sara opened her fan, smiling and nodding to a couple of her acquaintance who had come into the room. Then she turned her attention back to her companion, "And I must tell you I am far from being amused. I find your presence distasteful and insulting in the extreme."

His face was stiff, and his manner so cold and detached as to cause her further dismay. She had the oddest sensation that in speaking thus she had erred. "I apologize, Miss Auden," he said. "I can do no more than beg your forgiveness. If it were possible I would remove myself from your presence but to do so would be an insult to your brother and the other members of your family who have bid me welcome."

Her lips curled derisively. "I understand your scruples. Indeed I am delighted to discover that you have them."

He continued to study her face while she acknowledged the bow of one of her guests. "I don't believe I deserve quite *that*," he said softly after the man had gone. "No disservice has been done to you, Miss Auden, and I assure you none was intended."

"That is true but I believe that to be due entirely to my own rational behaviour. I only wish," she added in a harsh whisper, "that I were able to hand you over to the law."

To her astonishment he threw back his head and laughed, causing several people to stare at them curiously. "I hardly think my foolhardiness merits such harsh treatment, Miss Auden, and although I know your opinion of me could not be lower I cannot believe you would enjoy seeing your father's heir languishing in Newgate for so minor a crime."

The fan clattered to the floor to be retrieved by a passing gallant. She pressed it to her lips, closing her eyes momentarily. "Farley! Oh, no. Pray don't tell me Farley is involved in such roguery."

The laughter danced in his eyes. "But of course. You must know he was. Naturally it was only a lark; nothing serious was intended and I had hoped you would never know of it. You must forgive him his folly—and mine also."

She closed her eyes once more. "Never. How can you speak so lightly of a matter so terrible." She jumped to her feet in the most unladylike way. "I feel unwell. I must go to my room. Please excuse me, Lord Melford."

He got to his feet too and placed his hand upon her arm. "Before you go to the vapours in the privacy of your room, Miss Auden, a word of warning." When she looked up at him a chill tremor of fear ran through her bones. The amiability, the sardonic amusement, was gone and where, in her foolishness, there was once a look that thrilled her, his eyes now held a dark expression which frightened her. "Your brother may have been foolish and you may find my presence in your home distasteful, but I am here as Farley's guest and I cannot leave. I don't wish to and that's the truth." His eyes held hers in their thrall. "Knowing your awareness to his folly will only be a torment to him, for he is inordinately fond of you, so it would be foolhardy of you to mention this to your brother or to anyone else. Your discretion is required, Miss Auden; nay, it is demanded, and I beg you to exercise it for all our sakes."

She shuddered at the threat she read into his words and nodded dumbly. A moment later she was hurrying away from him, aware that his eyes were upon her until she was out of sight, and there seemed an endless path before her room was reached.

Once inside that blessed sanctuary Sara flung herself across the bed, sobbing loudly in her grief and fear. It was all so much worse than she had imagined. It seemed incredible that Farley should be involved in such treacherous acts, and yet she had noticed the change in him. His clothes, his manners, were all so mature, something she had put down to his affection for Genevieve L'Estallier alone. Now it seemed probable that his affection for the *emigré* had come later. A man like Farley, who had always been an impressionable boy, would be easy prey for a man of experience such as Richard Merrick. Farley would be easily persuaded to become involved in something he would regard as both exciting and romantic.

The sky was lightening by the time the first carriages began to rumble away from Beechleys. Sara was still awake, sitting dry-eyed by her window, watching the carriages bearing away their tired owners. She twisted her damp handkerchief unconsciously between her hands. The headache that she had used as an excuse to leave the gathering had now, because of all the tears she had shed, become a reality. She would have to endure the next few days as best she could, yet even when Melford's visit was over Sara knew she would spend the rest of her days fretting over Farley whenever he was out of her sight. If only she had held her tongue, had played Melford's game according to his rules, she would never have known of her brother's involvement. But spoken she had, and in doing so had uncovered such ills that must equal those in Pandora's Box. And never again would she know contentment.

Chapter Five

The first person Sara set eyes upon the following morning was her erring brother. For a moment she was tempted to blurt out a recrimination; to acquaint him in no uncertain terms of her knowledge of his involvement with Melford's nefarious schemes, but on recollection, remembering the look she had seen in the earl's eyes, she quickly changed her mind.

"Just taking some liquid refreshment down to the billiard room," he said as he made to go past her, making it plain that he did not wish to be detained for so much as a moment.

"Is that where your friends are?" If Farley noticed her cool tone he did not betray the fact.

"Good players—all of them. Must go, Sal, don't want to miss my shot."

"Just one minute, Farley." He stopped again at the command in her voice. "Do you gamble?"

He looked more than a little surprised and then recalled that this was his sister, not some simpering miss. "Of course I do. I have a great fondness for hazard; whist too, come to think of it."

"Then you must lose quite considerably."

"As much as I win," her brother admitted cheerfully.

Sara's handkerchief was twisted in her hands. "*Are* you in debt, Farley?"

"Good grief, no! What gave you that impression? I'm not that much of a fool, y'know." He pulled at his biscuit-coloured waistcoat. "Do I look as if I'm being dunned?"

Sara smiled. "Forgive me, dear. I didn't mean to pry, only . . . if you were in any . . . any kind of difficulty, you would come to me, wouldn't you?"

"There's no one else I *could* come to," he answered soberly, which touched Sara. He was a full year older than she, but owing to the responsibility she had shouldered at so early an age, he had always somehow seemed younger.

He turned to go again and she said quickly, and more harshly than she had intended, "How well do you know Melford? I've heard mention of your other friends on several occasions past, but you've never mentioned the earl, and he seems quite considerably older than you."

A telling flush spread up his pale cheeks and Sara felt a stab of dread inside her. He was standing in the hall, just beside the portrait of their mother, and just then, his eyes large and very blue, he looked so very much like her.

"Melford," he murmured. "Yes, well, I've known him for years. Yes, years. Haven't I mentioned him?" His tone was light but his flush deepened and he couldn't meet Sara's eyes. "Odd, I was sure I had, but then you've been away so much lately." He laughed in an over hearty way. "Great fellow, Melford."

He rushed off before she could detain him further with her unwelcome and embarrassing questions. Sara watched him go, her spirits sinking even lower. Now she was in no doubt there was some guilty relationship between Farley and Melford. The earl had a hold over her brother and she was quite helpless to intervene. She was persuaded that the Earl of Melford, behind his handsome face, distinguished lineage and exquisite manners, was a thoroughly wicked and depraved human being who would not scruple to betray her brother to the law should the urge overcome him.

Angelina's footfall on the stairs caused Sara to turn around and smile bravely. "I didn't expect to see you down so early," she said.

"It's not so early," Angelina pointed out. "Aunt Phoebe says she won't be down before dinner. The poor soul isn't used to such routs." She peered into Sara's face. "Neither are you and you do look pale, Sara. You should have stayed in your room this morning. You must be fatigued. Has your headache gone? It was very noisy, wasn't it?"

"The headache is much better, Angelina. You know I cannot abide staying in bed late." Sara opened the door to the small drawing room, a room conveniently situated on the ground floor. It had been furnished some years before for the family's use, and for economy of lighting and heating at Sir Henry's insistence. Sara was delighted to find that the room was empty. A small fire had been lit as the weather, although clement, was still rather chill.

"Was that Farley I caught sight of as I came down the stairs?" Angelina asked as they went inside. "I hardly expected to see *him* before dinner either."

"Yes, it was Farley," Sara answered heavily and, forestalling what must come next; "He's in the billiard room—with the others."

Angelina did not appear to delight in this revelation but a moment later she clasped her hands together joyously. "Wasn't it the most wonderful party, Sara? I wasn't obliged to sit out one dance."

Sara smiled at her sister as she leafed, rather listlessly, through a recent fashion magazine. "I'm glad you enjoyed it, dear. Everyone else seemed to do so also."

"And imagine! The routs and balls and breakfasts I shall be attending in London are far better. Far, far better. Oh, I can hardly wait. Sara!"

Sara stared at her sister. "That will undoubtedly be so, but I hardly need to remind you that you must behave at all times with the utmost decorum. To act the hoyden will not commend you to the highest ranks of Society, Angelina. I was shocked when you requested the waltz to be played. It may be quite acceptable in London amongst the ton, but here it is still regarded as fast."

Angelina's lovely mouth formed itself into an unbecoming pout for a moment or two. She was never one to take criticism easily, but neither was she depressed for long and a moment later her face dimpled into a smile. "Oh, Sara! I had no idea you were so . . . prudish. Miss Pringle, whom you must know is a most awful prude, made a point of congratulating me on my footwork when it was over. She said she had never enjoyed watching anyone more, nor seen a handsomer couple than the lieutenant and myself. Besides," she went on, her smile broadening, "you waltzed yourself, and with Melford. He certainly went out of his way to pay his attentions to *you*."

Annoyed at the way her cheeks coloured at the mere mention of his name Sara said quickly, "Nonsense. It would have been extremely rude of him had he not engaged me for a dance."

"But, Sara, two dances in succession! And I believe I am right when I say he sat with you in the supper room for a full fifteen minutes."

"And previously to that he danced with you and spent a great deal of time talking with you. He may not have spent so much time with me had you not been so much in demand elsewhere."

Angelina, despite herself, jumped up and down in her seat, laughing loudly. "Oh, I do believe you're right. He did tell Margaret that he con-

sidered the Audens to be an uncommonly handsome family, and one member particularly so. Meg
pressed him further on *that* score but he wouldn't
say more."

Sara felt nauseated. Angelina was just as impressionable as her elder brother and, therefore,
both were easy prey for the Earl of Melford.

"It was kind of him I'm sure," she answered in a
voice not quite steady, "but you must remember,
dear, that His Lordship must be sated with beauty
and that he's a notorious rake and a shocking flirt.
It wouldn't do for you to take his attentions at all
seriously."

"I do believe you are more of a prude than Miss
Pringle. Of course Melford is a rake and a flirt. I
hope I am not too naïve to realize it, but rakes and
flirts do marry eventually and Aunt Phoebe says he
must needs be in search for a wife."

Sara groaned inwardly at Aunt Phoebe's loose
tongue. Angelina stood up and curtsied prettily.
"My lady," she said with a giggle as she did so. "I
think I would make a wonderful countess, don't
you? Imagine receiving an offer of marriage *before*
my come-out. That would set the tongues wagging,
don't you think?"

"I think you would be better employed improv-
ing your sewing, your pianoforte playing and your
deportment, rather than indulging in such nonsensi-
cal supposition," Sara snapped.

Angelina's smile faded. "Oh, don't be cross, Sara. I was only funning."

"I'm glad to hear it," her sister replied. her countenance softening. "You really mustn't allow a man of experience such as Melford to turn your head. When you make your debut in Society you will have many men of rank paying court to you, and you must learn how to accept their attentions in a sophisticated way."

"I will," Angelina answered, "but you must allow it was nice to have the handsomest, richest and highest ranking man in the room paying one attention. I don't know how you could have allowed a mere headache to prevent you from staying. Nothing short of a seizure would have sent *me* to my room. Each time Melford stood up with me or spoke to me Jenny Colman was quite green, you know. He can't be quite that bad, Sara, if he took time out to speak to Margaret. He cannot hope to have a flirtation with her. She's quite taken with him."

"Only remember," Sara pointed out, keeping her head bowed to the magazine in a most uncharacteristic way, "that when you are in London you will meet many men, some of them with greater fortunes than Melford and higher rank, and Aunt Phoebe has great hopes of you becoming no less than a duchess. She knows of several likely young dukes in search of a wife."

Angelina's laugh echoed around the room. "I must see that she isn't disappointed."

Sara allowed herself a tiny sigh of relief and put the magazine, which in truth she hadn't been reading, aside. She picked up her sewing in a desultory way but for once her stitches were too large and uneven. She became aware that her sister was looking at her speculatively and Sara gave her an encouraging smile.

"Did you never mind missing your debut, Sara?" she asked.

"I've never had much of a chance to consider it," her sister replied. "I've always enjoyed keeping house for Papa and attending to the wants of you all. I never craved a social life beyond Beechleys as you already know. Margaret never missed it either, come to that."

"Margaret always intended to marry John. Had she gone to London she would have pined for him, but I should hate not to be able to go myself."

"But you *are* going."

Angelina continued to study her sister. "Charles Hanley is in love with you," she said abruptly. "Did you know?"

The needle jabbed into Sara's finger and a bubble of blood appeared on her skin. "I suspected as much," she murmured, watching her blood stain the white linen. "Although I think that love is too strong a word to use where Mr. Hanley is concerned."

"Does it matter what he, or you, would call it? A little encouragement and he'd offer for you."

Sara's head jerked up. "Offer for me! I don't want him to offer for me. I should have to refuse him if he did."

"Oh, why, Sara? He's a very nice young man and he cares for you deeply. You'd make a wonderful wife for a man of the cloth."

"I don't love Mr. Hanley and I don't want to marry him."

"There are times, Sara, when I'm out of patience with you. Do you wish to remain on the shelf?"

Sara had a sudden vision of Richard Merrick and closed her eyes tightly to blot it out.

"I know what I shall do!" her sister exclaimed a moment later. "When I am settled and have an establishment of my own I shall set about finding a husband for you. There must be many a man, a widower perhaps, who would fall for you on sight. You're so eminently sensible, Sara, and so good with children."

Sara recalled the widower in Harrogate who had been in search of a mother for his seven children, and she shuddered. Before all this recent talk of marriage she had never given much thought to it for herself, only now did she realize that she had no intention of ever becoming a wife simply to be a good housekeeper or the mother to someone else's children. And daunted by her sister's refusal to cooperate on a matter of such importance Angelina flung out of the room, leaving Sara to her unwelcome thoughts.

On reflection Sara did not know how she endured dinner that night. Her only consolation was that there were many others present apart from the earl and herself to help make it more bearable. And to give him his due, although he spoke to her for politeness's sake, when the circumstances decreed it, he did not go out of his way to press his presence upon her.

Sitting at the head of the table as she was accustomed to doing, facing her father at the far end, she was unavoidably placed next to the last man in the room with whom she would have wished to have been seated. From the slightly sulky expression on Angelina's face as the meal commenced it would appear that the young girl was not happy at the arrangement either, but before long she was engaged in conversation with Lieutenant Matthews who never failed to bring a smile to her face.

Sara's thoughts were far away. She picked at the plate of mutton before her, noticing with barely concealed resentment that the earl was eating a hearty meal and enjoying her father's best claret.

A mention of a name uttered in her aunt's shrill voice startled her out of the depths of her thoughts. "Sara and I had the most dreadful experience on the journey down from Harrogate." She was addressing Melford who was attending to her with interest. "I travel badly, you know, and it became necessary to stop for a short while. I didn't want to, of course, but my niece insisted that I should, and in such matters I own that she is usually correct." Aunt Phoebe paused to draw breath and Sara felt a horror of apprehension as she went on, "And whilst I was recovering we were held up! That rogue Bill Kersey. Bold they call him and bold he is. A more insolent fellow I never met."

Sara flashed a horrified look at the earl but his expression revealed nothing but sympathy. He turned to Sara. "What an unnerving experience for you, Miss Auden."

Sara looked down at her plate of untouched mutton in confusion. The man was a fiend to tease her so.

"It was appalling," her aunt added. "The rogue had the impudence to kiss Sara's hand and to flirt with her! I tell you it's impossible to be safe on the highway even in these days."

The earl lifted his wine glass and, casting a look at Sara, remarked, "Yes, indeed. The highways are still lawless despite the success the Runners have had at arresting those highwaymen who infest them. Unfortunately there are still those who evade capture."

Sara looked at him from beneath her lashes as he sipped at his wine and his calm amazed her. The man must be a greater actor than Mr. Kean, she thought.

"The shock, Melford, almost made an end of

me," her aunt went on, helping herself to a generous portion of rabbit pie. The continuance of the subject was, to Sara, an excruciating pain, but her aunt seemed insensible to it. "But my niece behaved very well, although," she added, stealing a glance at Sara before attacking her food, "I cannot help but think the shock of it has overset her sensibilities more than she will own."

"You go on a great deal about nothing," Sara said, finding her voice at last. "The man was polite, well-spoken and did not steal one penny from us."

"But the humiliation of it—to be at that fiend's mercy!"

Melford allowed his glass to be refilled and accepted a slice of lamb on to his plate before looking at Sara thoughtfully. "I have heard tell that Bill Kersey is very much the gentleman with a decided penchant for the ladies who cross his path. As you are both uncommonly handsome ladies," he smiled at the blushing widow, "you were fortunate to escape so easily."

Sara made a choking sound as she forced a forkful of meat into her mouth. She looked fearfully at her brother at the far end of the table but Farley was too deep in conversation to be aware of the subject under discussion at the other end.

"So we realize," Aunt Phoebe said in a subdued tone. "I have heard stories that do not bear recounting; but I cannot agree with my niece that he may be of high birth."

He glanced apologetically at Sara. "Miss Auden, in her distress, was most likely mistaken." He leaned back in his chair, staring at his glass thoughtfully for a moment or two. "But, of course, well-born highwaymen are not unknown. It is possible that he may even be an aristocrat."

Sara's fork clattered on to her plate. He was so obviously teasing her, enjoying his presence at her father's table, and all the while . . .

"Jem Tollett, you may remember, was discovered to be the fourth son of a baronet when he was arrested," he added.

A sound escaped Sara's lips and as it did so her aunt looked at her sharply. "Are you unwell, my dear. You're deathly pale."

"Talk of highwaymen upsets me, Aunt. I must be more affected by our experience than I had realized."

Melford was immediately concerned. "Miss Auden, accept my apologies. If I'd known such talk would upset you . . . but, of course, I should have appreciated that such an experience would shatter all but the most hardened sensibilities." To all at the table, save Sara, his voice held nothing but true concern, but she knew better. She couldn't help but feel that behind that mask of solicitude he was laughing at her.

"It seems that your appetite, also, has been affected, Miss Auden. Allow me to pass you some of this lamb. It would tempt the most jaded palate."

Sara wordlessly allowed him to transfer a slice to her plate whilst Aunt Phoebe eyed him with an approval she deplored.

Angelina, at the sudden realization that her sister was receiving far more than her fair share of attention from their most honoured guest, smiled prettily and said, in a way that seemed much too familiar to her sister's sensitive ears, "I hear that poor Mr. Brummell has been forced to flee, Lord Melford. I fear to fall foul of the Regent must ring a death knell to any man's place in Society."

The earl transferred his languid gaze to the perfect features of the youngest Auden girl. "That is true of most men, Miss Auden, but where Mr. Brummell is concerned he held his own court. His downfall is due to a more prosaic reason—gambling debts that he had no hope of settling. Having borrowed where he could he was unable to repay his debts of honour. That, Miss Auden, I'm afraid is the real cause of his flight."

"What a pity it happened before my come-out. I should have liked to have made his acquaintance."

The earl allowed himself a smile. "There were few enough who were afforded that honour."

Angelina's eyes were wide and Sara, determined not to be defeated by the man, struggled heroicly to to eat her dinner. "Were you acquainted with him, Lord Melford?" she asked.

"I was not one of his set, but I do know him; yes,

indeed I do. He was always fond of whist and I've often played a hand with him."

"I seem to remember," put in Lieutenant Matthews, "that you were once seen in the window of White's with the Beau. An honour indeed, Sir!"

"Indeed," the earl replied and Angelina's eyes opened even further. "Such an invitation was not to be refused."

"Poor man," murmured Angelina. "How dull Calais must be compared to London and Brighton, and how dull London will be without him. It seems that so many of the interesting characters have all departed for the continent. I should have liked to have made acquaintance also with Lord Byron, only he has gone too."

"And good riddance," her aunt added. "He has treated poor Annabella atrociously, I hear."

"I have heard that there isn't a clean bed to be had in the whole of France," Margaret commented, catching the end of the discussion.

"Byron is undoubtedly insane," Farley interpolated, adding with indignation, "But Mr. Brummell ran out on a debt of honour. He deserves his exile. All this talk of steam carriages is far more disturbing."

"If there's anything in the idea," Lieutenant Matthews said with a laugh, "it will mean an end to the Hussars. However hard I try I cannot envisage a charge upon a steam horse!"

Everyone laughed, even Sara who always found the lieutenant amusing.

"You have little to fear, I think," Aunt Phoebe informed him. "There will be few enough people persuaded to travel in a carriage without a horse, and bellowing in a much more fearsome way than a whole team. Although on a second consideration an engine will not be so careless as to break a foreleg on the Great North Road."

Aware that the earl's attention was being diverted again as he offered Sara a plate of cheesecakes, Angelina said, "Lord Melford, is it really difficult to obtain vouchers for Almacks? I live in a constant quake that I shall not be able to procure one."

"My dear Miss Auden," he replied in that easy way that infuriated Sara, "for one so fair there can be nothing to bar the way into even the most exclusive of company."

Much to Sara's relief the interminable meal was coming to an end. Gratefully she got to her feet, together with the other ladies, leaving the men to their port and talk of sport.

Chapter Six

The weather dawned fine and dry the following day and although in one way Sara felt it might encourage her brother's friends to remain, in another it enabled them to be out of the house, and thus out of her sight. Not that Sara objected to Farley's cronies; she had come to like Lieutenant Matthews very much and Tom Cheviot, Robert Booker and Desmond Adams seemed pleasant enough, if rather young and silly in her eyes. Had it not been for the presence of the Earl of Melford Sara would have been more than enjoying the present company, just as Angelina was doing. Beechleys was alive and noisy, just as it should be, and Sara was once more surrounded by the family she adored.

During the days that followed the rout, whilst Sara, her aunt and sisters received the various callers who came to Beechleys, the young bucks spent much of their time in the billiards room, sometimes fishing in the trout stream that passed through the estate, or racing their curricles along the narrow country lanes, startling the inhabitants who were used to a more peaceful pace of life as they did so.

One morning Sara came down to find six men crowded around a window. "What on earth is out there?" she was forced to ask.

It was Lord Melford, tall enough to remain at the edge of the group who turned to answer. "When we came down for breakfast, Miss Auden, Mr. Cheviot espied two flies on the pane. We are now waiting to see which one reaches the top first. I am holding the stakes and I believe Mr. Booker and Lieutenant Matthews will be the winners of this race."

After which Sara was forced to admit that men of fashion would bet upon anything.

In the evenings Sara and Angelina took turns in playing the pianoforte or singing the newest ballads, and on these occasions Angelina was rather more eager than usual to display her accomplishments in the field of music. When Sara, too, was persuaded to play a bagatelle on the pianoforte invariably it was Melford who would spring to his feet and offer to turn the pages for her, an act, she was sure, that was designed to annoy her, as indeed it did. It must amuse him, she was convinced, to force her to be polite to him. Usually, after tea had been served, presided over by Aunt Phoebe, the men more often than not would play a rubber of whist whilst the ladies embroidered or read the latest novels. *Pride and Prejudice* was favourite with Sara; she had been given a copy on its publication and never tired of reading it. Angelina, however, had just discovered Mrs. Radcliffe's Gothic novels and much to her aunt's disapproval had obtained a copy of *The Sicilian Romance*.

After three days of such rustic activities some of Farley's guests said their goodbyes and to Sara's relief, one morning before she was up, she heard the clatter of wheels on the drive heralding the departure of the young men and their respective manservants. Her relief, however, was short-lived; Lieutenant Matthews had accepted Farley's invitation to prolong his stay and, having no pressing engagements elsewhere, so had Lord Melford.

Sara was furious, although from her cool civility to the earl no one but he was aware of it. At first she was certain his decision to remain and enjoy a way of life that must be, to him, boring in the extreme, was due entirely to his perverse nature; she was convinced that he wished to tease her further and to enjoy her discomfiture whenever they were in each other's company. But then she became aware of another reason, and one that alarmed her far more—Lord Melford was paying marked attention to Angelina.

Angelina herself blossomed under the rival attentions of the earl and Lieutenant Matthews and did not even turn sulky when the earl stood up to turn the pages of her sister's music of an evening. After all Lieutenant Matthews eagerly offered to turn the pages for Angelina and such rivalry could only, the girl was quick to realize, encourage his lordship's suit.

Of course Lord Melford did not pursue Angelina in an obvious way—he was by far too much the gentleman to do that—but he was always around the hall whenever Angelina felt in need of some exercise in the garden, or when the vases needed replenishing with the roses that made the glorious display for which Beechleys was justly famed. Naturally Angelina, being a very human young lady, quickly realized this and her promenades in the grounds became even more frequent until her sister, much to Angelina's chagrin, realized the fact too and also decided that she was in need of air, exercise, flowers, and so on. Angelina accepted the addition of her sister's company with grudging good grace; being a well-brought up young lady there was nothing else for her to do, but her coolness towards Sara indicated her frustration and anger all too well. Lord Melford apparently welcomed Sara's presence and addressed the sisters equally. Being forced, as it might be said, into his company in this way did nothing to improve Sara's humour, or her opinion of him. So it was, on frequent occasions, a rather puzzled Lord Melford who escorted two ill-humoured young ladies around the gardens.

On those occasions when she was spared the earl's company Sara spent much of her time in the open air whilst the fine weather held, as out of doors she was more likely to avoid any contact with the man who was causing her so much anguish on so many different scores.

In the past she had always used the extensive grounds as a refuge whenever her responsibilities became too heavy. Now the abundant gardens laid down by her great-grandmother a century earlier, became her refuge once more.

She would walk down the paved paths beneath flower decked pergolas and rustic arches, or on the Chinese bridge across the artificial lake. There she would ponder upon the unfortunate circumstances which had brought the Earl of Melford into their lives. The more she considered the problem the more she was certain Farley did not participate in the actual robberies, especially as the earl had admitted the crime had been a minor one. But involved he undoubtedly was and when the villain was captured, as captured he must be, he would, she was sure, denounce her brother too. For days Sara had wondered if she dared send an anonymous message to Bow Street to inform them of where their most wanted quarry happened to be. Now she had reached the conclusion that to do so was impossible for three practical reasons, one being that she would have to obtain a wafer for the note from her father and that would bring the betrayal straight home to her. The second reason was, of course, her consideration for Farley's safety, and the final and most important reason against such an act was that she had not one shred of proof to offer.

Lord Melford was a diabolically clever man, and it came as a further shock to Sara to realize, after several days in his company, that the thought of him languishing in so filthy a hole as Newgate to be sent eventually to his death there, was as painful to her as was his presence at her home.

And his presence was painful. It was all too plain that Angelina, in her naïveté, would fall beneath his spell. Even to believe that his pursuit of Angelina was an honourable one gave Sara no comfort. Melford, Aunt Phoebe was convinced, must needs be on the look out for a likely wife now that he had inherited an earldom; in Sara's jaundiced eye she guessed he might seek to satisfy his odd sense of humour by marrying Angelina. She was certainly beautiful enough to gratify his discerning taste and was of good family, and it would be another way of ensuring Sara's discretion.

Sara had spent many a sleepless night, turning such a possibility over in her mind and she knew with certainty that she simply could not bear to see her sister married to that man.

Again, on such a score, she was deep in thought one still, hot afternoon when a footstep on the path startled her. She had left Angelina in the safe company of her other sister and the two of them had been poring over catalogues of cloth in the drawing room. Initially Sara had come out to cut fresh flowers to replenish the vases of Beechleys but having filled her trug with as many blooms as it would hold she had surrendered to her preponderance of thoughts and had sat down on a bench to stare unseeingly at an insect which was darting in and out of the rose bushes. She would have been glad to see Melford spend the rest of his days undetected as the dreaded highwayman rather than see him married to her sister. Angelina was always a sensitive child, and if she ever had an inkling . . . or, as to be expected, he quickly grew tired of her naïve charms once an heir to the title had been begotten, Sara was afraid that a girl of such delicate sensibilities might even lose her reason. Before she could become uncomfortably aware of another reason why the idea of a match between her sister and the Earl of Melford should be so abhorrent to her a pair of hesitant footsteps jolted her out of such danger.

Sara looked up and was surprised to see the figure of Charles Hanley approaching her. She summoned up a smile for him, not forgetting the embarrassment he had suffered on the night of the rout and that she was, in part, the cause of it.

He smiled too at such a welcome. "Good afternoon, Miss Auden," he said, his voice almost a whisper.

"It is a good afternoon, isn't it?" she responded with warmth. It was suddenly delightful to be in the company of one who caused her no anguish whatsoever. "Please sit down, Mr. Hanley. You must have had a lengthy walk, for I recall you dislike riding, and I am sure you cannot have come in the gig to arrive from that direction."

She removed the trug and he eagerly took up her invitation. "In truth," he said a moment later after casting his eye in an obligatory way across the flower beds, "I had hoped to find you alone, but did not sufficiently believe in such luck coming my way. I hope my appearance did not startle you. I fancy you looked rather taken aback."

"A little only, I assure you. You would be unwise to come out of your way when the path across the fields is such a short one." She hesitated a moment, looking at him curiously. "I recall that you mentioned something about hoping to find me alone, Mr. Hanley . . ."

"Yes, indeed." His face reddened slightly more than usual. His high colouring had not been improved by his walk from the vicarage in the full glare of the sun. She looked at him questioningly as he cleared his throat. "Miss Auden," he went on after several moments, "we have been acquainted now for many years—ever since we were children, have we not?"

"That is so."

"You must know, Miss Auden, that I hold you in very great esteem."

"And I you, Mr. Hanley," she murmured, folding her hands demurely in her lap. Dear as he was there were times when she found him a trifle tedious.

The young man cleared his throat again. "Oh, Miss Auden! That makes me the happiest of men."

She looked at him sharply as he continued, quickly, the words tumbling one over the other, "My admiration and respect for you has always been great, but even more so after you were forced to take over this vast house and supervise the upbringing of your younger brothers and sisters with no thought for your own comfort or pleasures. It was a monumental task and one you fulfilled admirably. That is why I have bided my time, Miss Auden. We have both been chosen for special work and must place our own wishes in the background. You must know I am to get the living in Nettleworth this autumn and, eventually, my father's living too. I had hoped to wait until I was settled—it is the only proper thing to do—but I feel," he took a deep breath, swallowing convulsively, "that your brother, Miss Auden, to be blunt has not repaid your devotion . . ."

At the mention of Farley's name the knowledge of what must surely be coming was blocked out of her brain by a new fear. "My brother, Mr. Hanley? Pray what is it you have to say about him?"

"Forgive me, Miss Auden—Sara." His skin took on an even deeper hue. "It is wrong of me to mention it, I know. If it were not for you—my regard for you—I would not have spoken of it." He drew himself up. "I am well aware of the manners of the fashionable young man and can only be glad that I have been given enough faith to resist those evil temptations myself. I appreciate that your brother is of age and perfectly entitled to use the house, which he will one day own, in whatever way he wishes, but my conscience would not rest easy if I were to allow you to remain here while Mr. Auden brings his depraved associates into your company."

Sara felt almost limp with relief. Charles Hanley only wanted to save her morals. For a moment, for one wild moment, she had feared that he had known about Melford and Farley's involvement with him. It was plain now that this matter had affected her nerves.

"Oh, dear Mr. Hanley," she said, smiling with relief, "I am in no danger I assure you. All Farley's friends have treated me with the utmost civility."

Mr. Hanley frowned severely. "That is not what I have observed."

Just then Sara caught sight of two unmistakable figures walking down a parallel path in the general direction of the ornamental lake. Sara stiffened again, her companion's lips narrowed into a disapproving line. Angelina's laugh rang out as Melford inclined his head to hers and spoke. When the pair became aware of being observed Angelina waved gaily whilst her companion inclined his head slightly towards them, and Sara watched them disappear from sight beneath an arbor of honeysuckle.

Charles Hanley turned to Sara again, taking her hands in his. "You cannot hold yourself responsible for them for ever, Sara. You have done everything possible to ensure their moral good, but the time has come for you to discharge an obligation to yourself—and to those who care for you deeply."

As she looked at him she was angry that tears pricked her eyes. What is happening to me? she wondered. My feelings have been inconsistent ever since I met that wretched man.

"Please Miss Auden, my dearest Sara, will you do me the honour of becoming my wife and make me truly the happiest of men?"

She continued to stare at him and then, after many moments, she realized her hands were still imprisoned in his. She freed herself from his hot and sticky grasp. "Marry you?" she echoed in a whisper, hardly knowing where to look. "This is quite surprising, Mr. Hanley. I had not thought . . ."

"Surely you knew of my regard for you, Sara."

She shook her head. "Truly I did not."

"Please, don't answer now. But consider, our marriage can be harmonious. I know you share with me a deep concern for the poor of the parish. I believe, with you beside me, I can work hard to ease their lot and do the work that the Lord, in his wisdom, has seen fit to bestow upon me. We live in wicked times, Sara. We must do what we can to re-furnish the lack of morals wherever we can."

Sara put two trembling hands to her face. If she hadn't been so involved in thoughts of Angelina and Farley she might have had some warning of this.

"I hope that I may always be concerned for my fellow human beings, Mr. Hanley," she said in a less than steady voice. She looked at him again and hated to see the hopefulness in his eyes. "Have you spoken to my father?"

Her heart beat unevenly until he said, "Not yet. If only you will give me one word of encouragement, Sara, I will speak to him immediately."

"No, you must not!"

His face registered shock. "But Miss . . . Sara, you said . . ."

"I said that I had regard for you, Mr. Hanley, which I have, please, believe me. But the question of marriage does not arise, nor ever can. I don't love you."

Charles Hanley could not have been more shocked. "I do believe you have been affected by the ways of these young bloods already. We have always dealt well together, you and I, and we have many interests in common. Many a marriage has been based on less."

Sara looked away. "I'm sorry. I had not meant to hurt you, but a marriage between us is impossible. I would make you a very bad wife."

"Permit me to be the best judge of that. I have never seen you conduct yourself with other than the utmost propriety. In all honesty, Miss Auden, I have never looked to any other woman. All I ask is that you don't refuse me out of hand and also that you do not affect a flirtatious air."

Sara could almost have laughed at the thought of adopting a flirtatious attitude to such a prosaic young man. Oh, what a wicked woman I am! she thought.

"Pray accept my refusal as a final one," she said in a steady voice. "I would be heartless indeed to offer you hope where there is none. And if you have any regard for me at all I beg you not to speak of this to my father."

Charles Hanley, a disappointed man, got to his feet and bowed stiffly. "I cannot look upon your refusal as final, Miss Auden. But I will say no more of it for now. I appreciate that matters of family needs must occupy all of your thoughts at this present time, and rightly so. In the meantime I hope you will always look upon me as a good and faithful friend, which I hope I am."

Sara only managed to nod her head as Charles Hanley went back the way he had come. In the silence after his footsteps had died away Sara stared ahead unseeingly. His proposal had upset her and not just because of the pain she had caused him in refusing. The pain nagged around her heart; it had done for days. She should have been aching for Charles in his disappointment, which unlike the young men of fashion and address could not be hidden behind a laconic word or a languid expression, but instead of his anguish tearing at her heart it was a picture of two perfectly matched people, one tall and dark, the other small and fair.

They had made such a beautiful picture, strolling along together. The sound of Angelina's laughter as she had responded to a word from Melford pierced Sara's heart, and at last she buried her face in her hands and cried.

Chapter Seven

When Sara caught her brother lingering over the breakfast table late the following morning she could hold her tongue no longer.

As she entered the breakfast room, tensing as she always did for fear that Melford would be there, Farley looked up and gave her one of the smiles that almost melted her heart. "Good morning, Sal. I haven't seen much of you these past few days, which is odd, for I came home for your sake."

His eager smile faded as his thoughts obviously transferred themselves to another, less welcome plane. At the sight of that expression Sara's spirits sank. "You've been busy," she said, seating herself opposite him. "Too busy to realize, no doubt, that your friend, Melford, is paying marked attention to your youngest sister."

Sara watched him as he digested this information. The expression on his face reminded her quite painfully of the dismay on Charles Hanley's face the previous day when she had dismissed his suit.

"Angelina? Good Lord! I never intended *that* to happen."

"I'm sure you didn't," she answered, helping herself to a slice of toast, which in truth she really did not want.

"It's the last thing I want . . ." He suddenly caught himself up, adding quickly, "No wonder Matty's looking so sour."

"Angelina is young and Melford's title will appeal to her despite Lieutenant Matthews being the most amiable of young men."

Farley threw his napkin on to the table. "I *knew* it was a mad notion to invite him!" he said almost under his breath, staring with unwarranted ferociousness at the damask tablecloth.

"Why did you?"

Farley shrugged and avoided her eyes, which did not reassure his sister one jot. "Can't think why," he murmured, "except," he added quickly, "that he's a sporting fellow. Seemed to want to be invited." His countenance brightened. "Father would never give him leave to offer for her, if that's in his mind. If it's not it hardly matter if he flatters the silly chit."

Sara eyed him steadily. "I shouldn't underestimate Angelina. Father will give her her way if that is what she wished. And why shouldn't he? It would be an excellent match. Do you think that is in his mind, Farley?"

The young man considered for a moment. "Melford's no fool and let's be honest, Sal, he would have to be to want to marry our sister as she is now with all her talk of balls and dresses."

Sara studied her brother steadily for a moment. It was clear that Farley did not wish to consider Melford as a brother-in-law, which gave no rise to her hopes. If Melford had, indeed, been one of his close friends, being possessed of a title and a fortune, Farley would have been delighted at the news she had just imparted. As he was so obviously vexed Sara drew her own conclusions as to the reason.

"It is well known," she said coolly, "that where affairs of the heart are concerned people want for common sense." She hesitated a moment before adding, "I know why you asked him here, Farley."

As his colour deepened her heart ached. She had vowed not to speak of it, but more important than her fear of Melford was a desire for Farley to have someone upon whom he could depend.

"How *could* you know?" he asked.

"My dear," she answered softly, "I know *you*. I also know that Melford isn't one of your regular cronies. You had a reason for asking him here, didn't you?"

Farley swallowed convulsively. "I'm sorry, Sal. It was done with the best of intentions—just the once." Her relief was enormous. It was as she had hoped. "I swear I won't do it again. It was a darned fool idea anyway. It Melford hadn't turned up when he did I wouldn't have gone on with it. Forgive me, Sal."

She smiled and nodded, and hoped that in whichever way her brother had been accomplice to the highwayman on that one occasion it would never be discovered. For that they would have to rely upon the benevolence of the Earl of Melford, which did not reassure Sara overmuch.

Farley got to his feet abruptly, shaking his head in disbelief once more. "*Angelina.* Good grief, Angelina! I might have known it would come to this."

As the door closed behind him Sara drew a deep sigh. Voices, as Farley greeted someone outside the door, drifted to her ears. A few moments later when it had faded she relaxed again and poured herself a cup of luke-warm tea. It seemed that she was walking ever deeper into a maze.

Her duty was clear; she supposed, as on many times before, that she should denounce the rogue even though it would be a matter of her word against him. Her word was well-respected and that must surely count for something, she reasoned. It was even probable that Bow Street would be able to produce several other victims of the highwayman to bear witness also. But although Sara knew just where her duty lay it was no longer concern for Farley that stilled her tongue, if, indeed, it ever had been.

When the door opened some time later she turned to bestow a smile upon the newcomer, expecting that her aunt or one of her sisters had at last come down to breakfast, but when she saw that it was the sole occupant of her thoughts these past five days—and more—her cup clattered into the saucer instead.

"Good morning, Miss Auden. Clement weather, is it not?"

Sara muttered an almost inaudible answer, but he was unperturbed by her lack of warmth, and as he commenced to help himself to several cutlets and a generous portion of roast beef she watched him from beneath her lashes. Dressed in a coat of dark blue superfine, which seemed almost moulded to his shoulders, and pale yellow pantaloons which displayed his well-shaped legs to perfection, she thought him—in all honesty—an attractive man.

When he turned and caught her eyes upon him he smiled and in confusion she looked away again. He seated himself across the table where a fresh cover had been laid and when she looked up again he was attacking his breakfast with marked unconcern.

Sara got to her feet. "I shall ring for fresh coffee, my lord."

He leaned across the table and caught her hand. "Please be seated, Miss Auden. The coffee will wait. I am not addicted to it, so, please, finish your tea."

Sara sank down again and helped herself to another slice of toast, which was as much as she could manage this morning. She wished to excuse herself from his company, yet she delayed doing so. It was only rarely that she came upon him alone and suddenly she was assailed with a hunger of curiosity.

He looked up to find her studying him once more and this time she did not look away. "I trust you are enjoying your stay," she said but could not rid her voice of its harshness.

"Indeed I am, Miss Auden," he replied warmly. "And your father and brother have each been good enough to say that I should be welcome to call here whenever I wish." He frowned momentarily. "But I am afraid the burden of visitors has been wearing on you, so soon after your return. If I may be permitted to comment, you seem a trifle pale."

"We have always been known for our hospitality at Beechleys, my lord, and on several occasions past we have had many more visitors than we have here at present."

"Then perhaps it is the humidity that is wearing, Miss Auden. So many people cannot bear it. Your sister, I collect, is one such person."

Sara's cheeks began to flood with colour. "I enjoy this time of the year. The gardens are always at their best."

"I'm thinking that their magnificence is entirely due to your ministrations."

"My mother planted the rose garden but I do supervise its care." She looked directly at him. "I wouldn't have thought you so interested." Her tone was challenging.

"But I am," he answered mildly. "Our gardens at Melford Park are also very beautiful but Beechleys, I think, has the edge. It must be the woman's touch. Roses, particularly, respond to it. My own mother devotes little time to her garden. She would rather entrust its care to the gardeners we employ. A mistake obviously."

"Was it your interest in gardening that prompted you to have my sister guide you around ours yesterday?"

"Yes, she was kind enough to offer. We looked for you to join us, of course, but were unable to find you. You were, we discovered, with the gentleman I met at your rout the other evening, and we thought better of interrupting what looked to be a private conversation."

She lowered her eyes again. "You refer, of course, to Mr. Hanley. He is an old friend of the family."

"Of one particular member it would seem."

Her eyes remained firmly fixed on her plate. In fact several seconds later Sara realized she knew exactly how many crumbs lay on it.

"You must excuse, Lord Melford, what might appear to be over zealousness on my sister's behalf," she said breathlessly; his presence always caused her to be short of breath, "but it is on account of our having no mother. I am, in a way, responsible for her and, Angelina, being so fair, is a constant worry to me. She is about to embark on her first season and although her portion is genteel it is far from being considerable."

Her warning was as awkward as it could be and must be obvious to him. She only wished she were as smooth with words as he and could have warned him off in a more oblique way, only panic had suddenly urged her to do something to prevent a calamitous happening.

"I am sure, Miss Auden, that you have little cause for concern. Your sister's small portion will in no way detract from her social success. As you say she is fair of face and any man in earnest will not be deterred by so trivial a matter."

Sara made to get to her feet, but his hand restrained her yet again. "Please, Miss Auden, can we not be friends at last?"

"I think you know we cannot," she replied, trying ineffectively to release herself from his grip, "but I hope I have been as civil to you as I would be to any of my brother's guests."

"Civil yes," he replied, an unusual bitterness creeping into his tone, "but warm no."

Her eyes remained on her imprisoned hand. "I wish I had the courage to denounce you publicly. Perhaps one day I shall, only it will be when we are in a company where my disclosure will be of the utmost effect."

"You are at times, Miss Auden, quite like a

child," he snapped. "If you had one ounce of so-phistication in you you would realize that what has happened is not an uncommon occurrence. In fact even today it is quite commonplace. At the present time few people know of it. Your brother and my-self will certainly never speak of it, which leaves you, and surely you must know that any mention of this matter will only heap humiliation upon your-self."

She gasped at the implication of his words and her eyes rose to meet his as he said, "There will be no more talk of public denouncements. It is not a matter for gossip. That I require your silence for my own sake needs no mention but equally I do not wish to see you hurt, Miss Auden, as you will be if this matter becomes public knowledge. Do you un-derstand what I have been saying?"

His tone was clipped; so cold that she shuddered involuntarily. His warning could not be clearer. She wondered how far he would be willing to go to en-sure her silence. Farley's discretion was assured by the mere fact of his implication. No doubt the earl possessed proof of it to be so sure of himself.

"I understand you perfectly," she answered in an uneven voice, "but knowing how I feel I cannot help but believe you remain here just to tease me."

"Tease you!" he exclaimed, laughing loudly. "Oh no, Miss Auden, I do not remain here for that."

The door opened. His voice had been sufficiently loud to mask the sound of footsteps outside. Angelina stood inside the doorway, her aunt and sister, Margaret, behind. Angelina stared at them both, her expression a mixture of outrage and bewilderment.

Sara managed to pull her hand free as Aunt Phoebe said in an impatient voice, "Go on, girl. We cannot stand in the hall all morning."

Angelina quickly recovered herself. "Good morning, Sara," she said with a quick, acid smile in her sister's direction. "You are, indeed, an early riser this morning." Without waiting for a reply she went straight to the table and sat down next to the earl. The acid quality of her smile had disappeared as she gazed at him with her blue eyes wide. "What a pleasure it is to see you at the breakfast table, my lord."

"I find that breakfast is a most congenial meal when it can be shared with four such charming ladies as there are present today."

Margaret smiled good-naturedly at such extravagant flattery. Sara was vexed to find that Margaret dealt well with him. She was the one person whom Sara believed would remain indifferent to Melford's nefarious charm.

Aunt Phoebe and Margaret had placed themselves across the table to the earl and Angelina. Aunt Phoebe helped herself to some toast and said to Sara, "Don't just stand there, dear, ring for Maitland. We need fresh coffee and hot toast."

Sara silently did as she was told, aware that the

earl was watching her, a frown marring his handsome features. She was suddenly afraid. He was worried about her, doubting now her discretion, as he might well do after her near-hysterical outburst. Fervently she hoped that such doubts would not provoke him into drastic action. He was ruthless, utterly ruthless, she had no doubt of it now. He needs must be ruthless to survive the dangerous double life he was leading.

Certainly she hadn't meant to be so outspoken and vowed to curb her tongue in the future. The trouble was, being a straightforward person, she was used to speaking her mind. But she must remember that this was not only the fourth Earl of Melford, he was also a member of a band of men renowned for their heartlessness. If caught he would hang, so he might even be tempted to do away with her to safeguard himself and his family honour. At these extravagances of thought she almost swooned. In fact she did sway on her feet but steadied herself on the mantel before her discomfiture could be detected.

Aunt Phoebe and Margaret were chattering with unconcern whilst Melford contributed with his usual ease of tongue. When Sara turned round again Angelina was looking at her coldly and when Sara lowered her gaze her sister said in a loud, flirtatious voice, "Did you not wish to join my brother and Lieutenant Matthews fishing this morning, Lord Melford?"

"Indeed I did, Miss Auden, only unfortunately I have some urgent business to execute at Melford Park and I must take my leave of you all without further delay."

Angelina's face was a picture of dismay but Sara could hardly restrain her joy. He had known he was leaving all the time! She quickly crossed the room again as the butler and a maid arrived bearing fresh food and drink. She sat down at the table once more for fear that her legs would no longer support her. It hardly mattered now that he had enjoyed his sport with her. He was going and Angelina could recover from her infatuation.

"I do hope you will come again, Lord Melford," said Aunt Phoebe, a forkful of roast beef hovering close to her mouth. "My nephew and Lieutenant Matthews have announced their intention of remaining here until the end of the month, after which they will, of course, be removing to Brighton."

"I do thank you, Mrs. Carnforth," he answered, bestowing upon her his charming smile. "It's good of you to be so welcoming." His eyes slid to Sara and away again. "I appreciate it, but unfortunately I may be involved in estate business until I, myself, remove to Brighton. I have promised to escort my mother to the Regent's first rout."

Angelina was staring downcast at her plate, and Sara's heart went out to her. However, she was consoled that Lieutenant Matthews was remaining for a time, the reason for which she was fully aware, and when Angelina embarked upon her social season she would undoubtedly attract a score of suitors.

The earl glanced at Angelina, a smile softening his face in a way it never did when he looked at Sara, a realization which shocked that lady profoundly. "Should I not be able to return before that time I will be honoured to be your first caller when you arrive in London."

Angelina looked up, smiled and blushed as her aunt replied, "You will be most welcome," and then; "How does your mother do?"

"She is very well. She is leaving Melford Park for Brighton within the week to prepare our house there; that is another reason I must leave here. I didn't know that you were acquainted with her, Mrs. Carnforth."

Aunt Phoebe smiled slightly. "It was a long time ago. I recall that the countess was a very vivacious person."

Lord Melford smiled too. "In that she has changed very little."

"Aunt Phoebe was considered to be quite a beauty in her day," Margaret put in and as her aunt blushed Melford replied smoothly, "In that *she* has changed little."

It was some time later, having completed her household duties in a somewhat preoccupied manner, that Sara collected her sketching block and went outside. She found a spot in a secluded little corner where she hoped she would not be disturbed for some time. Sketching was something in which she was rather accomplished. Normally she enjoyed the pursuit but today, somehow, the short, light strokes refused to compose themselves into any recognizable shape.

She wondered where that inital delight at Melford's departure had gone, for she had been unable to maintain it for many minutes. Suddenly the house seemed very empty without his impressive presence. Without realizing it she had enjoyed even the bitterest exchanges that had occurred between them.

It was here that Phoebe Carnforth came across the woebegone figure of her eldest niece and as she approached Sara looked at her guiltily. Since the night of the rout she had been avoiding most members of her family for fear of betraying the sinister connection between Farley and the Earl of Melford. Sara was unused to deceit so she decided to avoid contact with those who knew her well, who may be able to detect that something was amiss.

"So this is where you've been hiding yourself," said the widow as she seated herself next to her niece. Sara did not miss the note of censure in her voice.

"You must know that I enjoy the weather, Aunt Phoebe. When we have the rain, the fog and the snow there is ample opportunity to stay indoors."

"It's a bad habit. You'll ruin your complexion. Angelina never ventures out into the sun without her parasol and neither should you. You're fortunate enough to be able to wear gowns of such light stuff. When I was a girl we had to wear gowns of heavy silk and brocade—none of your muslins and calico—and certainly no decolleté for the men to ogle."

"On the contrary, Aunt Phoebe, in the portrait of Mama, which hangs in the hall for all to see, her neckline is exceedingly low and revealing. Besides men don't ogle me," she added in a dull voice. "You should save your criticism for Angelina, not that it matters. When you buy clothes for her coming Season she will have to wear the latest fashion and whatever the depth of decolleté it must be so."

"I've no doubt we can find a compromise," her aunt answered grudgingly.

Sara looked at the widow and said, somewhat peevishly, "I trust you haven't joined me out here to discuss the latest fashions."

"No, indeed. Your sister has brought to my notice a grievance which she has been harbouring, as you may well know. She feels you are trying to come between her and Melford. She complains that each time he walks with her you go along too."

"But of course," Sara looked perversely down at her shoes. "His lordship has no objection. I am sure he wouldn't want to jeopardise Angelina's reputation before she has been introduced into Society."

"Stuff and nonsense," Phoebe Carnforth retorted. "There can be no harm in him walking with her in the gardens of her own home."

"I had my reasons, Aunt Phoebe."

"No doubt they were admirable ones. However, it would have been better if you'd allowed him his chance to make her an offer of marriage, had he wanted to."

Sara looked aghast. "That was the last thing in his mind, Aunt Phoebe. It surprises me that you are foolish enough to even harbour such a thought. You said yourself he was a flirt, and worse. I have noticed also that he has a malicious sense of humour. It might suit him very well to amuse himself with an innocent like Angelina and then, when he goes back to London, to destroy her reputation with a few well-chosen words."

Aunt Phoebe looked shocked. "Oh no, dear. No, Melford wouldn't do that. A flirt and a rake he may be, but he is also a gentleman and he wouldn't do that after accepting the hospitality of Beechleys."

"Just because you were in love with his father, Aunt Phoebe, it doesn't necessarily follow that Melford is a gentleman."

Mrs. Carnforth fussily adjusted her shawl. "Who told you I was in love with him? What nonsense to be sure."

A smile softened Sara's fierce expression. "You were, weren't you?"

"Perhaps a little. There were few enough girls

who weren't a little in love with Harry Merrick at some time or other. He married Ariadne Bethington—a great beauty there's no doubt—but she didn't possess an ounce of common sense. I daresay that is why Angelina has taken his fancy. I recall very well," she went on with a chuckle, "on one occasion—I think it may have been at Vauxhall—her feathers were so high that they were caught in a lantern." She chuckled again. "It took two footmen and three magnums of champagne to douse the flames."

Sara, despite herself, could not help but laugh at the picture her aunt's words had painted. "Oh, dear," she gasped, wiping her eyes on a scrap of handkerchief, "I do hope she didn't come to harm."

"Well it could easily have been so. She was in the family way at the time and Melford was born within a week of it happening—prematurely I've no need to add. He was a sickly babe too, so I understand. It wasn't expected that he would live long enough to inherit and poor Ariadne was in despair because her next two were girls. You wouldn't believe that now when you look at him." She gave a sigh. "But I dare say you're right, Sara; he wouldn't have offered for Angelina now even if he'd been given the opportunity." Sara looked at her aunt hopefully. "She's too young and he must realize it. It will be much better if he waits until she's had her come-out. It will suit him far better to wait until then. I'm sure he's the type of man who would prefer to wed a beauty acknowledged by the ton rather than an obscure country miss."

Sara felt too miserable to murmur anything other than, "Do you really think so?" and before she could prevent herself, "I do hope not."

"Don't you fancy being sister-in-law to the Earl of Melford then?" Aunt Phoebe asked, laughing anew. "I must own that I would rather be aunt to a duchess or a marchioness, but I'd be content to see Angelina settled with an earl and there's the truth of it."

"It is not the title I object to, Aunt," she answered in a stronger voice, "but the man himself." Mrs. Carnforth stared hard at her niece and Sara had to look away. "He's not at all the man I would wish for my sister."

"And why not, miss?"

Sara took a deep breath. "Oh, I don't really know. Angelina is such a sensitive child. I'm not at all sure she would like to be the last of a string of loves."

Aunt Phoebe gave a hoot of laughter. "As long as she *is* the last. Oh, Sara, show me a man who hasn't had a string of loves and I'll show you a man not worth having." She hesitated a moment, her laughter abating a little. "You don't mean to tell me you have a fondness for him yourself?"

Having the bald truth spoken so loudly threatened to shatter Sara's precarious composure even further, but her reputation for keeping a calm head was not undeserved. It was true enough though. The words Aunt Phoebe had so carelessly flung at her were no less than the truth. She had fallen in love with Richard Merrick, alias Bill Kersey, and never was there a more ill-starred affection.

"Nonsense," she said in a shaking voice.

"My dear," Aunt Phoebe murmured in a gentle tone, "there is no shame in such feelings. You must not be afraid to admit you are like any other female and share a tendency with them to fall in love with a handsome man."

"I am not in love with him," she insisted. "I am not a chit just out of the schoolroom to be taken in by his pretty speeches."

"No, indeed dear," her aunt answered, smiling complacently. "At least you are not a chit just out of the schoolroom. You are a mature woman, are you not?"

Goaded beyond all reason Sara retorted angrily, "I had hoped not to speak of it whilst he was still a guest here, and I hope I have hidden it well during his stay, but the truth of it is, Aunt Phoebe, I dislike him excessively."

"Now you do surprise me."

When, a moment later, Angelina appeared, clad in a cool morning dress of white calico with the low neckline of which Aunt Phoebe disapproved, Sara was a little more than relieved.

Angelina twirled her parasol in a dispirited way,

which forced her aunt to say tartly, "If you insist on frowning in such a way your face will retain that peevish look. And do put up that parasol—higher! I cannot get your sister to understand that a burnt skin is most unattractive, but I have no intention of removing to London with a chit who has a brown face."

Sara looked up. Angelina's face was as milky white as always, her skin with the bloom of a peach. Sara's heart ached unbearably. There could be no lovelier woman in the whole of Society.

Angelina sank down between her sister and her aunt, shooting Sara a dark look as she did so. "Well, Melford has gone," she said, peering at her toes, clad in satin slippers, "and may not be back, although when he took his leave just now he promised to try and return while Farley is here."

"You will be sure to see him in London," her aunt said in a rallying tone.

"But that will not be for months. And by then he may have become entranced by someone new."

"In such a case you may well count yourself fortunate," commented Sara, hating herself as she spoke. "There are far better men to be had."

"What do you know of men?" her sister challenged, with the air of a great sophisticate.

"Never mind, dear," Aunt Phoebe broke in quickly. "Lieutenant Matthews is still here."

"He is *only* a lieutenant in the Hussars."

"You think far too much of your own consequence," Sara snapped. "Only a lieutenant indeed! He was commended for valour at Waterloo."

"He is the third son of Viscount Langley, you know, dear. An old and respected family, if not an influential one."

"Does it matter?" asked Angelina, dismissing the subject of Lieutenant Matthews as unimportant. "They're racing their curricles to the village," she went on. "Of course there can be no comparison between Melford's greys and Farley's and Lieutenant Matthews's cattle. I asked to sit up beside Melford but he said that, as I would undoubtedly bring him luck, it would be unfair to the others. Farley and Lieutenant Matthews won't be back until dinner; they're going to a cockfight at Nettleton." She stole a glance at her sister. "So from now on, dear Sara, you will have no cause to seek my company. I fully expect to be allowed a promenade around the garden on my *own*."

"Don't be such a child," Sara snapped. "You have yet to make your debut—don't I know it! The talk has been of nothing else since we returned. I declare that even life in Harrogate was less tedious.

"If I had allowed you in Melford's company alone a reputation for being fast may well have preceded you to London."

"Fast!" scoffed Angelina. "What a prude you are to be sure. You're jealous—quite jealous," she added airily. "You cannot bear to see Melford paying his attentions to me."

At further truths being unconsciously uttered the scene in front of Sara's eyes swam with red. "Jealous!" she cried. "Why you foolish little child, don't you realize to a man like Melford you are just a plaything, an object with whom he can amuse himself?"

Angelina's face flushed darkly as Aunt Phoebe said, "Now children, please! This is a most unseemly display by two young ladies of breeding."

Sara, too choked with anger and jealousy to speak, could only point a shaking finger at her sister. "It is your youngest niece who needs a lesson in what is seemly," she gasped at last.

"She *is* jealous," protested Angelina. "She's afraid I will receive an offer of marriage before she does." She turned back to Sara, smiling maliciously, "If you want to bring Charles Hanley up to scratch you will have to propose to him yourself."

Sara's hand flashed out to Angelina's face and she saw with horror the red mark her slap had bestowed upon that fair cheek. Angelina screamed and, holding one hand to the offending cheek, ran back to the house, sobbing heart-brokenly.

"Really, Sara, there was no need to do that. What on earth is getting into you, my girl?"

Filled with horror and remorse, Sara bit back a sob and jumped to her feet. "I must go to her. Oh, poor Angelina. What have I done?"

Aunt Phoebe pulled her down on to the seat

again. "Leave her a while. It will do her no harm to reflect a little upon the folly of a waspish nature."

Sara put two hands up to her own flaming cheeks and turned to her aunt. "I am not jealous, Aunt Phoebe. I'm not!"

Aunt Phoebe smiled. "No, dear."

At the sight of her aunt's complacent smile she added quickly, "Charles Hanley did make me an offer of marriage. If I so wished I could be announcing my betrothal now."

Aunt Phoebe's smile faded as Sara knew it would. Already she was regretting the proud impulse that had urged her to speak of the matter. "Why have you only just spoken of it? Your father has said nothing."

"Charles didn't speak to Papa. Charles always likes certainties so he wanted to be sure of my acceptance before he spoke to Papa."

"Oh, my dear, I'm so pleased for you."

Sara looked up sharply. "But, Aunt Phoebe, I refused him."

"And quite rightly too. It doesn't do to accept a man's first offer. My mother always insisted that it was improper to accept either of the first two. Not that I would go so far as to say that . . ."

"If he proposes a further fifty times I shall still refuse him."

"How can you be certain of that? I must say I am most disappointed in you, Sara. Charles Hanley will obtain a very good living. His cousin is Lord

Denvoe, and Charles is a nice-looking, nicely-behaved young man."

Suddenly Sara gave a little gasp of exasperation and, jumping to her feet, she cried, "I'm so tired of all this talk of marriage. It's becoming quite a bore. I'm only glad I shall not be coming with you to London, for I am convinced that the females there will talk of nothing else either!"

She finished on a sob and burying her head in her hands she flew back towards the house, in the wake of her sister, leaving her aunt to stare after her in astonishment.

Chapter Eight

It was some time later that Sara managed, in the privacy of her room, to stem the profusion of tears her outburst had brought forth. She glanced critically in her dressing mirror at her blotched and swollen face and when she was at last reasonably composed she changed her gown, which had become slightly crumpled, and put on instead a new one made of chintz.

She had to knock several times at the door to Angelina's bedchamber before she received permission to enter. The curtains had been drawn across the window, and as they were of velvet they blotted out almost all of the light. As she entered the chamber Sara could only just distinguish the form of her sister, laid out upon the bed. She went across to the window to allow in more light, after which she could see that Angelina was laid across a pillow with a cold compress pressed to her cheek.

Sara went across to the bed and, sitting on it, said in a soft voice, "Let me see how bad the damage is, my love."

Angelina perversely refused to look at her sister,

but knowing that Sara was more than adept at healing minor ills she allowed her to examine the inflamed cheek.

"If I'm permanently scarred," she warned in a thick voice, "I shall never forgive you."

"There will be no permanent damage," Sara promised in the voice that had soothed her sisters and brothers through many a childhood complaint. "But you would be quite right in not forgiving me. I don't deserve your forgiveness."

Suddenly Angelina flung herself into Sara's arms, sobbing anew. "How could I say such things to you, Sara? I must be very wicked indeed."

"No, love," her sister replied. "We are, neither of us wicked, but nevertheless we must bear this in mind as a lesson for the future. It is very wrong to lose one's temper and say hurtful things."

"I was dreadfully provoking I know. I am much to blame as you, Sara. It will never happen again. No man will ever come between us, Sara. Never. Whoever he may be."

Sara smiled at her naïveté. "It's to be hoped that a man will come between us eventually. Nothing could be more natural or desirable." Her smile faded slightly. "But he must be the right man. Yes, he must be the right one." She hesitated a moment before adding carefully, "And I cannot believe Melford is the right man for you."

"I wish you would like him, Sara. I cannot be happy if you don't." Her wide blue eyes, still awash with tears, searched Sara's face hopefully. "He really is the most splendid person I have ever met."

Sara's smile remained on her face despite the ache in her heart. "Remember, you have had little chance to meet other people of the ton, Angelina." She hesitated again. "My dearest hope is to see you married to a man of good birth who will make you happy. I am not convinced that Lord Melford is that man. I pray you won't do anything rash before you have had at least one Season. If Melford is in earnest and your feelings true ones, then there is no harm in waiting. That is all I ask, love."

Angelina smiled. "I should hate to miss my Season, although as a married woman I could enjoy all the routs and balls just as well; even more so with a husband to escort me rather than Aunt Phoebe." And on seeing Sara's stricken face added quickly, "Oh, I'm only teasing, Sara. I do know of Melford's reputation as a flirt. It's very flattering for him to pay me his attentions whilst he's here, but that doesn't add up to an offer, nor, I think, is it likely to now. Even if he did offer for me I would be honour bound, on behalf of my fellow women, to make his heart ache a little."

Sara was in a small way reassured. Perhaps she had underestimated Angelina's understanding of the man. Had she, herself, not been aware of the earl's other identity, she too might have enjoyed responding to his charm or even indulging in a light flirtation.

Like two conspirators the sisters hugged each other tightly, laughing all the while. After a few moments Sara pulled away. "I'm ravenously hungry. Shall we go down to see if they've left us any luncheon?"

Angelina slid from the bed and as Sara smoothed her gown she said, her head slightly to one side, "That's a fetching gown, Sara. Is it new?"

"It's one of those I brought from Harrogate. Do you really like it?"

"Didn't I say so?"

"Then it's yours."

Angelina clapped her hands together in delight. "Oh, how good you are, Sara! I don't deserve to have such a sister."

Sara laughed and, sliding her arm around her sister's waist, said, "Let's go downstairs. I hope you realize we have scandalized poor Aunt Phoebe with our wanton behaviour."

"You can depend on it, Henry," his sister said in a doom-laden voice as she helped herself to a venison pasty, "your eldest and your youngest daughters are in love with Melford. Not that Angelina knows her own mind yet. It's Sara who's the problem. At her age it's no infatuation; it's a matter of permanency, not some passing fancy."

Sir Henry, at this revelation, almost choked over his pigeon pie. "Sara! Why Sara is five and twenty and beyond such foolishness." He levelled an accusing eye at the widow. "Did you put this nonsense into her head?"

Mrs. Carnforth pressed one plump hand to her equally plump breast. "I, Henry? I hope not."

"It's all this talk of marriage, and Farley's cronies making up to my girls. Sara always had a level head on her shoulders before she went up to you."

Phoebe Carnforth sat back in her chair. "I do believe you would have preferred me to die just so that you could keep Sara with you. You are an exceedingly selfish man, Henry.

"My goodness, what is getting into everyone today? It must be the weather. I'm quite off my food. I can only face one slice of mutton, to be sure."

"Better call the leech then," her brother retorted in a heartless tone. "Ah, here are Angelina and Sara now," he said as the door opened, adding to his sister's further mortification, "Nothing much wrong with them. Just look at 'em."

Now that the object of her desires and despair had removed himself from Beechleys Sara believed that life there would continue in its previous smooth way. But she was disappointed. Although Angelina was not, apparently, and to her relief, missing Lord Melford—Lieutenant Matthews was clever enough to prevent that—Sara herself missed him. She felt, plainly, miserable and several sleepless nights were spent on a tear-stained pillow.

"He's not worth pining for," she told herself

sternly one morning as she peered at her pale features in her mirror. "He'll come to his end on the scaffold with no one to mourn him and his name forbidden within his family." And as she spoke the tears fell again at the thought of the vital spark of life being choked out of him at the hands of the public executioner.

However, all was not black in Sara's world. Margaret and her husband showed no disposition to leave Beechleys and Sara, ever fond of children, spent more and more time playing with little Wilhemina whilst the child's nursemaid spent more and more time flirting with Wilfred Nettle, the second footman. The lively presence of Farley and Lieutenant Matthews, although diverting to Angelina, cheered Sara very little despite the fact that she tried. Even the picnic in the park, which every member of the family attended, failed to raise her spirits to any marked degree, nor did the several dinner and card parties to which they were invited over the next few days.

Eventually she realized that company was not the answer, so, early after lunch one day, whilst Margaret and Aunt Phoebe were resting and Angelina dared not venture out because of the sun, Sara took her shawl, her bonnet and her sketching block and walked down towards the ornamental lake.

The lake had been made in a hollow out of sight of the house as one of her mother's frequent fancies. The sight of the water was cooling and peaceful and the ridiculously useless pagoda on its far bank made a scene perfect for sketching.

Sara walked slowly down the slope towards the lake and spread her shawl on the grass beneath the shade of an old, old oak tree. The open vista, the untidy woods beyond the lake, where now the men were out shooting wood pigeons, were quite different to the formal gardens with their profusion of beds and orderly privets.

She settled down to sketch, feeling happier than she had done for some time. All was peaceful and as it had done so often in the past the pastoral scene put tranquillity into her heart. Some yards away one of the gardeners could be seen scything the grass and from the wooded land beyond the lake the sound of shots were occasionally heard followed by the excited barking of the retrievers, but even this could not detract from her calm on this afternoon. The pain in her heart was easing. It made the risk of contracting a chill from sitting on the ground seem insignificant. Falling in love with a rogue who may very well end his days in an unmarked grave was the first imprudent thing she had ever done, yet she was still sensible enough to realize that it could not hurt for ever—as long as he was never there to re-open the healed wound, as long as he didn't marry Angelina. There lay her real fear. She knew she couldn't bear to be aunt to his children, to nurse them through their illnesses as she had nursed her brothers and sisters, for she knew she would now never marry and bear her own.

The scene before her was one she had drawn and painted many times before and now her fingers nimbly flew across the block. As the picture took shape a feeling of satisfaction permeated her being. She held it at arm's length and as she did so a very familiar voice said, in a very familiar tone, "It's very good. You have a talent for sketching, Miss Auden."

She whirled round, squinting against the sun in order to see him and in doing so did not care that unbecoming lines would form around her eyes and upon her brow. He was standing several yards away and from where she sat he appeared enormous. Sara could hardly suppress the rush of joy she felt at seeing him again and could say nothing for fear of betraying it, so she turned back to her occupation again without saying anything at all. Her hands continued busily at her drawing, yet her mind was no longer on it. Since he had left Beechleys several days before, on each occasion that he had crept into her consciousness she had feared that at that very moment he was executing the robbery that would be the ruin of him. While he was here she need have no such fear.

"May I sit beside you?" he asked a moment later. Now he was standing at her side.

"If you wish," she answered without looking up.

"As long as you are not afraid of marking your pantaloons, or of catching a chill."

"I am neither a baby in need of coddling nor a dandy, Miss Auden," he answered in an amused voice, "so, with your permission, I will sit down."

All too aware of his unnerving presence at her side she began to embellish her drawing of the lake, bridge and their backdrop of woods.

"I didn't expect to see you here again, Lord Melford," she said when the silence began to be oppressive.

"My business was concluded far more quickly than I anticipated and I have also managed to see my mother safely on her way to Brighton."

At this latter piece of information she turned to look at him, her eyes full of amusement. "Safely? I do, indeed, hope so. You must know how dangerous it is to travel on the public highway nowadays."

"My mother always travels with armed outriders," he answered, returning her gaze levelly. "I gather your unfortunate meeting with a highwayman has made you particularly sensitive on the subject."

Sara felt a familiar anger well up inside her but Melford seemed unaware of it as he went on, "You may be interested to know that when I was in the Blue Boar yesterday I heard say that he held up the York Mail near Grantham the day before yesterday." So that was the real reason he left, thought Sara. Well, at least whilst he remains at Beechleys he is safe from the law and leading an honest life, she reasoned, although how it could be regarded as honest she didn't quite know. She warned herself never to lose sight of that fact; that his life was one constant lie.

"He was almost apprehended on that occasion," Melford went on, grimly Sara thought. "The Runners have intensified their activities in the area. I fancy he may not be at liberty for much longer."

"I sincerely hope not," she answered, looking away.

"Do you?" She knew he was smiling. "From what I have heard he affects the ladies in quite a different way—or," he added softly, "are you the type of genteel female who would enjoy the spectacle of a public hanging if they were still held."

She closed her eyes tightly. How could he tease her so! "I beg you, please do not speak of it."

"I'm sorry. It was cruel of me to tease you. It was not a pleasant experience for you."

When she opened her eyes the expression in his was truly compassionate. "Why, then, are you here?" she asked in a faint voice, attempting a safe and normal conversation. "Did you not wish to accompany your mother?"

"I will join her at a later date when the Season is under way. I preferred to return here just now."

She looked at him suspiciously. His lips curled a little. "One might almost accuse you of inhospitality in putting such a question to me," and he added quickly, "I had hoped to attend a race meeting later this week, and seeing your brother and Lieutenant Matthews also intend to go, it seemed convenient for me to return here and journey with them."

"If you wish to join them they are at present in the grounds shooting wood pigeons."

"Yes, I know." She wasn't looking at him so she did not see the wry smile that appeared upon his face. "If I join them, however," he explained a moment later, "I would have to change my clothes and at present my man has work enough unpacking my portmanteau."

She looked at him again. "You are most thoughtful."

"My servants and tenants are of the general opinion that I am a nice enough fellow."

His complaisance angered her anew. "Perhaps being servants and tenants, they are not in a position to know you truly."

Suddenly all amusement had gone from his manner. "But they are better acquainted with me than you, Miss Auden."

"I don't doubt it," she murmured.

He sat with his arms clasped around his knees for a few minutes, studying the pagoda across the small expanse of water. The breeze gently ruffled Sara's hair, blowing wisps of it across her face and causing her to brush them away angrily like tiresome flies.

"That's quite a remarkable construction," he commented.

"My mother planned it, together with the lake and bridge before she died—when the Prince made the Chinese style all the rage. You may have noticed that the large drawing room is done out in a similar style."

"We also have a room in such a style at Melford Park."

She dared to look at him then. The welcome breeze was blowing his dark curls about his head and just then he looked less formidable and not in the least dangerous. "Do you really?"

"Oh, yes. Your mother was not alone in her eccentricities."

His rueful tone made her laugh and his less alarming appearance made her more talkative. "I believe, from what I recall of my mother, we were fortunate not to have had the entire building redecorated in that style."

"I'm of the opinion that your mama and mine would have dealt very well together. Your pagoda, lake and Chinese bridge, however, are far more pleasant to look upon than our Gothic ruin."

Sara clapped one hand over her mouth to stifle a gasp. "You cannot mean it."

"I assure you I do. Perhaps you, your aunt and sisters would care to ride over and see it one day. It has to be seen to be believed. Its construction was almost the end of my father. If it hadn't been for Bonaparte he would have taken a Tour. Now Mama is a dowager she sees the folly of it, but there it is and there it must stay to blight the eyes of future generations of Merricks."

"I'm sure our respective mothers must have been acquainted, Lord Melford," she said, unable to stop laughing. It was hardly credible that such a man was the product of this zany parent. On a second consideration it wasn't so impossible; it would account for the undoubted crazy streak that prompted him to commit highway robbery.

"They very likely were. Is that a portrait of her I saw hanging in the hall?"

"That was painted by Mr. Gainsborough the year that Mama met my father. It's a very good likeness. Mama was fortunate to have her portrait done by Mr. Gainsborough, for he died very soon afterwards."

"You remember her well?"

"Anyone who ever knew her could never forget her."

"She was very beautiful, and that is something she was thoughtful enough to hand down to her children."

Sara twisted a blade of grass around her finger. How it would amuse him to know of her feelings. What a triumph for him. Silently she vowed he would never know.

"Only Angelina and Farley favour her. Meg, William and I favour our paternal grandmother."

"Then she, too, must have been a remarkably handsome woman."

"Did you see the group Sir Thomas Lawrence painted?" she went on quickly, the pitch of her voice far too high. "It's in the gallery. You must pass it on the way to your room. Of course William is not on it. He wasn't born then, and neither had Sir Thomas been knighted then. It's so fitting that the Regent should honour him with the accolade; he is truly a great artist. Heavens, how I do go on!"

"I enjoy hearing your voice." He waited a moment before adding in a much brighter tone of voice, "I had noticed the portrait and consider it a charming study. When you marry, your husband must commission a likeness of you to be done by Sir Thomas. I can envisage a portrait of you seated in a high backed chair wearing the . . ."

She looked at him sharply, "Wearing what, Lord Melford?"

He eyed her uneasily and it was the first time she had seen him in the least discomposed. "I was thinking that a collar of emeralds would become you." A moment later he asked thoughtfully as he stared ahead, "Did none of you ever, as children, take a tumble in that lake? It cannot be very deep, yet deep enough to drown a man or a child, and it is very near to the house for real safety."

"Pray do not put me in mind of a such a thing. We were never allowed far from the house without our nursemaids or governess, and later without a footman or groom, but now I perceive that it could be dangerous. It is as well it has only just come to my notice or I wouldn't have known a day's peace when the children were younger."

"I doubt if your mother considered the danger when devising the plan for it. I, myself, broke a collar bone once when climbing the ruin. It is a great temptation to little boys."

"I gather Melford Park is a much larger estate than ours."

"Very much so, Miss Auden. Your brother and father have both been kind enough to allow me to ride with them over the estate during my stay here and I must own that Beechleys is very well maintained."

"My father, and grandfather before him, were always as much concerned with the well-being of their tenants as with the profits of the estate."

"So I perceived. It does them much credit. The well-being of my own tenants, though they be tenfold those at Beechleys, has always been of the utmost importance to me. I do hope you will ride over before your aunt and sister remove to London. I believe you would like Melford Park. Some of the rooms have an historical connection which I fancy would interest you."

"We should like that very much," she found herself saying.

He smiled. "Then it is settled. When my mother returns she will issue an invitation, unless, of course . . ." He did not continue what he was about to say. Sara bit her lip; she could have completed the sentence for him. *"Unless, of course, Angelina is mistress there."*

She stared at him for a moment or two before putting to him the question she asked of Farley. "Have you known my brother for long, Lord Melford?"

"You may know he was my junior at both Eton and Oxford."

"Quite a coincidence."

A small smile played at the corners of his mouth. "Not really considering the number of young men who attend those establishments. My brothers went there too."

She looked up in surprise. "You have brothers, Lord Melford?"

His answering smile was a mocking one. "I have two, and two sisters also. You see? I am quite human after all."

She ignored his mockery, which she had come to expect, and continued to twist blades of grass around her fingers. "And how was it you both embarked upon this . . . scheme?"

She stole a glance at him from beneath her lashes. His eyes had darkened as she knew they would. She hated herself for speaking of something that invariably brought out the worst in his nature, especially now they were enjoying for once such amiable conversation.

"If you insist on knowing," he said shortly, "I overheard your brother discussing the possibilities of such a scheme. He was aware, of course, that it was, to say the least, a crazy notion, but it was there in his mind so I resolved to encourage him. There, I take the blame entirely."

"I never doubted that."

He stole a glance at her and then away again. "The scheme would have come to naught had I not pursued him to Watier's and engaged him in conversation. I was bored, in truth, so I allowed him to . . . involve me." He turned to look at her again. "It seemed an amusing diversion at the time, but had I known you would become involved in this way, believe me, Miss Auden . . ." He smiled sheepishly. "But you know that already. I cannot add more. Your brother was not in earnest and neither was I—not then."

He continued to look at her hopefully but she refused to look at him. He wanted her forgiveness, she knew it. He wanted her to be safely under his spell, but she refused him the satisfaction of seeing her succumb.

"I understand it is customary for young men of fashion to perpetrate many cruel hoaxes just for the fun of it."

"I was never one of them."

"No, my lord," she answered bitterly, "a mundane lark would never suit you." She turned to him suddenly. "I only hope that you do not regard my sister as an "amusing diversion.""

There was no reply for a moment and then he said, "You have nothing to fear on her behalf."

Such an ambiguous answer from his smooth tongue did nothing to allay her fears. She felt him capable of doing and saying anything that would benefit himself. She was afraid of him; not just for the damage he could cause her heart, but for the damage he could do to her family. If her father ever learned of Farley's implication it would kill him. He took such a pride in their good name, as, indeed, must do the Merricks.

She was aware of his scrutiny and although embarrassed she forced herself to meet his gaze. "Why do you smile so?" she asked.

"Because you have streaks of charcoal down your cheek where you have brushed away your hair."

In a flash he had taken out a handkerchief and would have wiped away the marks had she not started violently. "I have a handkerchief here," she murmured.

"Don't soil it, Miss Auden. Please allow me."

Within seconds the offending marks were wiped clear, yet he was still reluctant to let go his hold upon her. Sara's heart was beating loudly at his closeness. Her eyes remained downcast for fear that he would recognize the look in them.

"Please, Lord Melford, I beg you let me go."

"Sara," he said in a voice that was urgent and low.

She looked up eagerly, responding to his tone. "Yes."

The dogs were coming nearer. The noise of their barking along with the sound of masculine voices and laughter carried easily on the wings of the breeze across the still waters of the lake. As it reached them Melford released her. He got to his feet with an easy agility, the gold tassels of his Hessian boots swinging as he did so. Sara stared at them in fascination. "The shooting party is returning," he said unnecessarily.

"Then I too must return to the house to change my gown and wash my face," she said quickly in her confusion. "My father will not tolerate a shabby appearance, and my aunt will scold me for venturing out into the sun without a parasol and with uncovered arms."

He looked down on her from his superior height. "You look charming, Miss Auden, utterly charming." He bent down and handed her to her feet and whilst he retrieved her shawl and sketching block she was able to compose herself a little and even managed to give him a small smile of thanks when he straightened up.

He hesitated to hand her the sketch she had made. "May I keep the sketch of your pagoda. It is very well done and I should like it to show to my mother. Perhaps then she will not feel too badly about our ruin."

Sara laughed. "Please do, but it is by no means

remarkable. I do have several water colours of this scene, one of which you might like to have. I'm told I do them quite nicely."

"That, I imagine, is an underestimate of your talent, Miss Auden," and then as she murmured an embarrassed reply, "I should be honoured to have one. May I escort you back to the house?"

Sara glanced across to where the men had just emerged from the woods. From their light conversation and frequent laughter she guessed that the bag must be a good one. She could imagine Angelina's reaction if she were to arrive back at the house escorted by Melford. The last thing she wanted was a further estrangement from her sister.

"Please do not trouble, my lord. I know you must long to rejoin your friends. It will take me but a minute to reach the house."

Before he could reply she lifted her skirts and hurried up the slope. When she reached the top she glanced back and he was still standing in the same spot, watching her. She hesitated a moment, recalling in all its glory that moment when his face had been so close to hers, and then she turned away and hurried back towards the house.

Chapter Nine

Sara was not the only person to be glad that Melford was back, Angelina could hardly repress her joy at seeing him too, and witnessing this occurrence Sara's heart sank. Her hope that Lieutenant Matthews had replaced Melford in her sister's affections foundered then.

But there were also those who did not welcome his return. Aunt Phoebe, to Sara's astonishment was one of them. Of course her behaviour towards him was impeccable but Sara had spent almost a year in close company with her aunt and had come to know her well. Perhaps, Sara mused, Aunt Phoebe really was determined for Angelina to marry a man of higher rank—silly as it seemed to Sara for any man, be he a prince even, to be more desirable as a husband. Perhaps, she speculated, Aunt Phoebe, having been exiled from Society for so many years was not anxious to be done out of supervising Angelina's come-out, or perhaps she had even come to the conclusion that Melford was simply amusing himself. Whatever Aunt Phoebe's reasons for her apparent change of attitude to Melford, selfishly, Sara welcomed it.

More predictable in his reluctance to welcome the earl back was, of course, Lieutenant Matthews. During the intervening days he had been the sole receiver of Angelina's favours, so it was understandable that he would not receive with enthusiasm a man he would regard as a rival. Farley's feelings were difficult to divine but Sir Henry, Margaret and her husband John, blissfully unaware of any undercurrents in the atmosphere, all greeted him warmly.

"You look rather peaked," commented Margaret late one afternoon as she and Sara sorted through some linen to be repaired.

"My complexion has always been pale."

"I didn't say you were pale. In fact your skin seems to have been touched by the sun to a small degree."

"You're getting quite like Aunt Phoebe. She is forever prosing on about the evils of the sun and the wind on the complexion, but I happen to like it."

Sara thrust the linen away with an impatient hand. Margaret and she had always been close; moreover Margaret had always been sensitive to her sister's moods. Today her instincts had not misled her. The moment Farley, John and Lieutenant Matthews had ridden off to visit some neighbouring farms belonging to the Auden estate the earl had appeared and somehow, within a space of minutes, had offered to take Angelina for a short ride in his phaeton and four, in which he had travelled from Melford Park.

Admittedly Angelina had been showing signs of fretfulness and boredom at the defection of one of her beaux and in other circumstances Sara would have welcomed having her diverted, but Sara did not believe that Melford's action was a kindly one. She pushed a renegade wisp of hair from her damp face and reflected on the evils of jealousy.

It was several days since that interlude by the lakeside. On reflection it seemed almost like a dream and she was often caught out, her thoughts reconstructing that precious time with him. No wonder he was such a success with women, she thought, angry with herself. None could be immune to his charm. She had often to remind herself that while Bill Kersey was also known for his charm he also abducted young women and ruined their lives. She silently vowed once more never to allow his charm to blind her to his evil ways.

Margaret walked across to the window and her sister, who followed her with her eyes, said, "My tongue is too sharp these days. I'm becoming a shrew."

Margaret laughed. "That you will never be, but staying in Harrogate with Aunt Phoebe must have been something of a strain, to say the least. It's no wonder your patience is not what it was."

"Really she's quite a dear, but I longed for you all, naturally, and Beechleys." She paused a moment. "How long do you and John intend to stay?"

"As long as John is happy to stay, if it isn't too much for you to bear with Farley and his friends remaining."

"You know that it isn't. I love having you here and I know you won't be hurt if I say I especially love to have Wilhemina here."

Margaret laughed again. "The Manor is comfortable, of course, and Mama-in-law is so kind and good, but I love Beechleys too. I've been trying to improve the gardens at the Manor but I don't seem to have your touch, Sara. And every time Mama-in-law sees me so much as savouring the scent of a flower she clucks and fusses so because of the baby. Nothing must jeopardize John's heir!"

Sara's eyes sparked with amusement. "So it *is* to be a son this time."

Margaret's eyes opened wide in mock-horror. "Indeed it is. I shall not be allowed to give birth to anything else!"

Sara laughed, knowing well Margaret's formidable mother-in-law. "It isn't as if Wilhemina isn't the most darling child in all the world."

"Well, if I present her with a sister this autumn it will not be my fault. I have done everything Mama-in-law bids to ensure the birth of a son."

"Surely she doesn't believe such nonsense makes the slightest difference, Meg."

"She certainly does. She vows that is how she got John, so how can I argue? She is very much the country woman. Seriously though, I'm not at all sickly as I was when I carried Wilhemina, so that must be a good omen, and Doctor Balfour is very pleased with me."

Their conversation was abruptly interrupted by the arrival of Wilhemina and her nursemaid. The child was carrying a doll knitted by Aunt Phoebe since her arrival and she thrust it into Sara's hands to be admired.

"It is a handsome doll, my pet," Sara crooned. "What's her name?"

The little girl babbled incoherently while her mother and aunt looked on fondly. Margaret glanced out of the window. "It's much cooler now. Shall we take some air, Sara? I'm in need of it, I confess."

Sara looked up. "I do so enjoy playing with your daughter, Meg. Must you separate us so soon?"

"Let's take her too. Come along, Dulcie, bring Wilhemina outside with us. The air will give her a good appetite and ensure that she sleeps well tonight."

Sara hurried to her feet. "It may be too much for you, and dear Wilhemina also."

"Nonsense. I enjoy a stroll. We won't be walking far, I trust. I took a great deal of exercise before Wilhemina was born, and a bonnier child I've yet to see—even if I am the one to say so."

"Very well," Sara said doubtfully. "Only don't let Aunt Phoebe know. She is bound to disapprove."

"Aunt Phoebe! She has never had a child. Doctor Balfour believes in excercise."

"My word," murmured Sara. "Whatever next?"

Hating herself for it, when they were outside, Sara glanced anxiously down the tree-lined avenue. Margaret caught her eye and she smiled sheepishly, saying, "Melford and Angelina have been gone quite some time. I do hope that there hasn't been some mishap."

"John says he hasn't met a better driver or horseman, so I think we can relax knowing our sister is safe in his keeping."

Sara was already well-aware of Melford's skill at the ribbons and astride a horse. It was not the fear of an accident that troubled her mind.

Automatically their steps were taking them towards the lake where the air was fresher than in the formal gardens which abounded with trees and bushes. Wilhemina and her nurse trotted on doggedly ahead.

"Did you visit here frequently whilst I was in Harrogate?" Sara asked.

"Several times, the last being at Christmas. I felt quite sorry for Papa. He is lost without you, you know. However, it was just as well. He will have to accustom himself to your absence and to Mrs. Jameson's presence when you are married and have your own establishment.

"Farley was home for a few days whilst we were here and Angelina invited a schoolfriend to stay to bear her company—a Miss Branscombe. She was an odd girl, not at all like Angelina. She was very plain and she hardly spoke a word. Each time Farley addressed her she blushed and stammered so. Farley grew so heartily sick of it he returned to London after two days."

For a few moments no more was said between them. Both watched the child who was sitting by the lake now playing with her doll. Margaret eyed her sister sideways. "Lately, Sara, you have had the look of a woman in love yourself. Do tell me. You know you can rely on my discretion. Did you meet someone marvellous in Harrogate?"

Sara laughed aloud out of relief. "I met several remarkable gentlemen to be sure, Meg."

"Dare I ask?" Sara's heart beat faster. Margaret had always been perceptive. "I saw Charles Hanley in the garden the other day . . ."

Sara drew a sigh, a mixture of relief and sadness. They had reached the lake and Dulcie was making a daisy chain for the child. "He did make an offer of marriage, but I refused him."

Margaret leaned against one of the supports of the bridge and held her sister's eyes until she lowered her gaze. "In truth I cannot say I am sorry. He's worthy enough, I dare say, but I couldn't fancy him as a brother-in-law. And I cannot envisage him as a husband for you."

Sara could have hugged her. "Do you know, Margaret, he made no mention of love, only his regard for me and then he cited our mutual concern for the parish poor! He didn't even speak to Papa; he wanted to be sure of me first."

Margaret smiled wryly. "That sounds exactly like Mr. Hanley. No, dear, it just won't do."

"Oh, Meg," said Sara happily, "I knew you would sympathize with me over this. You have so much common sense."

"So I've been given to understand," Margaret answered airily. "Maddening, isn't it? There are times when I would like to have a reputation of being deliciously madcap as was our darling Mama." She glanced at her daughter, now proudly wearing the daisy chain, admonishing her, "No, dearest, don't pull at your cap ribbons." She turned back to Sara, "Aunt Phoebe is of the opinion that Melford is in earnest over Angelina, and that was his reason for coming back so promptly. But I cannot believe that he is so foolish to want Angelina for his wife. I had thought him to be far more sensible."

"I do hope you may be right," Sara answered in a faint voice. "I don't believe it would do at all, Meg."

"Oh, look, Wilhemina is admiring her reflection in the water and Dulcie, the stupid girl, has wandered off."

Sara's head shot round and she was darting across the grass towards the child in a moment. It was almost as if she were seeing it through another pair of eyes. Only seconds had passed since she had dashed after Wilhemina, yet the moment she reached her the child's unsteady legs gave way and she toppled head first into the water.

Margaret cried out in dismay as did the startled nursemaid. Acting solely on impulse Sara reached out and grabbed hold of the baby's dress, hauling the sodden child on to the bank before she'd had a chance to slip beneath the surface of the water.

Dulcie, her face full of guilt, gathered the sobbing child to her as Sara sank down breathlessly on the grass. As the nursemaid tried to calm Wilhemina she also attempted to apologize for her momentary lapse in vigilance. Margaret cut her short, saying, "Mr. Plant will speak with you," turning immediately to her sister, "Are you all right, Sara? Heavens, I thought you were going to topple in too." Sara was too breathless to do anything more than nod. "Thank goodness you always keep your head," Margaret added.

Sara looked up at her sister. "Are you all right, Meg?"

"Of course I am." Sara turned to Wilhemina's erring nursemaid. "Take Wilhemina back to the house, Dulcie, before she takes a chill, and pay more heed to her care in future."

But the child, now ceasing to sob so heartily, realized that her doll had fallen into the lake too, and let out a howl, pointing one fat finger to the one colourful streak in the otherwise grey waters.

"You will have to send a footman or one of the

gardeners with a grappling hook, Dulcie, if we are to retrieve the doll. We shall certainly have no peace until it's recovered."

Sara, having recovered her wind, got to her feet as the child let out another howl of protestation. "That's why there is no point in waiting for a footman or a gardener," she observed. "I can easily get it. The lake's shallow enough."

"But not in the middle, Sara, so it's best that you don't try."

Sara laughed. "The doll is nowhere near the middle."

"You'll get yourself wet," Margaret warned, her voice unusually loud in an effort to be heard above her daughter's howling. "Oh dear, her voice, at times, is just like dear Mama-in-law's!"

"My dress is already mud-splattered, so I cannot possibly do more damage there, and I cannot bear to hear her cry so heartbrokenly. I recall that Angelina had such a doll when she was no more than Wilhemina's age and she was devoted to it also. This one may have sunk without a trace before anyone comes to retrieve it and then we shall know no peace at all."

"You may take a chill. It's not worth the risk, dear. Wilhemina has other toys."

"I never take chills," Sara said and with an air of purpose kicked off her shoes. Holding her dress clear of her ankles she put one foot into the water, which barely came up to her calf. She gave Margaret a smile of triumph and, saying soothingly to her niece, "Never fear, my pet, I shall have it for you in a trice," she stepped further into the water. But the further she went the further the doll floated away towards the middle.

She could hear Margaret shouting to her and her voice seemed far away. Sara shivered a little, for the water was cold despite the warmth of the day, and was seeping through her clothes at an alarming rate, tending to drag her down into the lake.

The doll was at arm's length. She realized then that the wretched article could easily have been reached from the bridge with a pole. It was foo late for that now; she had already reached it. Her arm stretched out to grasp it and as it did so her foot slipped off the ledge and she was floundering helplessly in the water. She tried to regain her footing but the shelf continually slipped away from beneath her feet. Time and time again the water closed over her head. Silently she prayed for help, at the same time hoping that Margaret would not take it into her head to stage a rescue herself.

Suddenly she became aware of someone in the water quite close to her. The water parted and she blinked it out of her eyes to see Melford only yards from her. He reached out for her and as he caught hold of her she was thrust under the water again. Her lungs were almost bursting. She thought she heard him say, "Don't struggle. You can do nothing yourself." But she panicked and even though she fought his iron grip with every last remnant of her strength she could not free herself. In her helplessness he could kill her so easily.

She wanted to tell him that she would rather have her tongue torn from her head than betray him, but it was too late for that. She attempted to speak but was only able to swallow a mouthful of water. The waters closed over her head for the last time and she saw only blackness.

When the blackness gave way to dark blue Sara heard the familiar voice of Aunt Phoebe. "Thanks be to the Lord. She is alive!"

Sara opened her eyes to a canopy of blue sky. The anxious face of Aunt Phoebe immediately loomed over her. "There, dear," she said soothingly, "you're back with us. For a moment I thought we'd lost you."

"So did I," Sara managed to reply, but her voice was harsh from all the water she had swallowed. "Are Meg and Wilhemina safe?"

"Perfectly, dear. I've packed them off to the house. What a silly thing for you to do."

Sara then realized that she was lying on the grass edging the lake. Her clothes were dripping with wet and plastered closely to her body.

"Don't you know the lake is deep in the middle?" Aunt Phoebe chided.

"Papa always said it was too shallow for fish."

Sara attempted to sit up but was defeated in her

objective. If there was one thing she hated it was being helpless. "The footmen will be here presently to chair you back to the house," Aunt Phoebe informed her.

"I won't be chaired anywhere," Sara said in a tearful voice, horrified at the prospect of doing something so undignified.

"All right, dear, but you must rest there awhile and recover yourself. Don't tire yourself any further."

Sara turned her head and her eyes alighted upon the form of Angelina who was staring back at her with wide and frightened eyes. "Oh, Sara," was all she could say in a voice full of tears as she pressed a handkerchief to her lips.

Sara tried to give her a reassuring smile but as she did so she caught sight of yet another figure nearby. He looked a giant from where Sara was lying. His Hessians were caked with mud as were his pale cream buckskin breeches, and his starched neck-cloth was drooping damply. His coat, which a master tailor had lovingly moulded to span those broad and muscular shoulders, was now lying across the upper part of her body shielding her from the wind. He was standing, arms akimbo, staring down at her. His face bore an expression that was uncompromisingly grim. His eyes met and held hers for eons of time and then Sara drew hers away, looking at Phoebe imploringly.

"Aunt Phoebe," she said in a faint voice, struggling, and at last succeeding, to sit up.

"Do you feel ready to go into the house now?" she asked, twisting her hands together in anguish. "The sooner the better, dear, I feel."

Sara shook her head and then beckoned Aunt Phoebe closer. Aunt Phoebe inclined her head to her niece's. "What is it, Sara? Can't it wait until you are in the house? If you remain here for much longer you will take a chill."

"I never take chills." She lowered her voice. "Aunt Phoebe, Melford tried to drown me out there."

Mrs. Carnforth laughed in a derisory way. "Drown you, dear? He saved you. He was the only man tall enough—and yes—brave enough to do it. Yes, truly. He acted most promptly. He saw it all from the avenue. Thank goodness his phaeton is of the high-perch kind. When you are more recovered you must thank him. You owe him your life."

Suddenly, as they had tended to do of late, Sara's tears began to flow again. "Oh, Aunt Phoebe, I've been such a chuckle-head."

The widow smiled. "Not that, love. Not that. Come along; let's go to the house and I'll get you into a dry nightgown and a warm bed. Than I shall make you some hot milk. This could be the death of you."

"It nearly was," Sara answered, sobbing convulsively.

It was such an unusual sight to see Sara discomposed to such a degree that Angelina turned to Melford saying in distressed tones, "Oh, Melford, what are we to do? She has lost her reason!"

The earl came forward and helped Sara to her feet. She murmured her thanks without looking to him directly. "You will want your coat," she said, "before it is ruined beyond redemption."

Before Melford could object to her suggestion Aunt Phoebe snapped, "You will keep yourself covered." When Sara looked at her she averted her eyes. "Your clothes are wet, dear. Very wet. I have heard of some shameless females who dampen their clothes purposely so that they show . . . so that they *cling*." She flashed an apologetic look at Sara, who could not help but smile to herself, and then added, "Come along then, dear, home to bed with you."

"I don't wish to go to bed," Sara protested. "All I need to do is change into dry clothing."

"I insist that you do. Do you wish to ruin your sister's first Season, for you will do so most certainly if you die? What do you say, Melford?"

"I think it would be unwise for Miss Auden to take any further chances on her health, and unwise to delay here also."

"Well spoken," agreed the widow. "Take Melford's arm, dear. Do you think there is no one else capable of supervising a few servants? Now you will do as you are told for once. Come along,

Angelina. We will go ahead to see that warmed clothes are prepared for your sister."

As the two women hurried ahead Sara stared vexedly after them.

"Now, Miss Auden," said the earl as he came up to her, "the breeze is becoming brisk. I think you should obey Mrs. Carnforth, for she is a lady full of common sense."

Sara started after her sister and aunt without so much as a glance in his direction, but Melford caught up with her almost at once. "Please take my arm. You would gratify that good lady by being so kind as to do so."

"I am quite able to make my way back to the house without support, Lord Melford," she answered, looking at him at last.

His face was serious but his expression was relieved by the amusement present in his eyes. "That is undoubtedly so."

"And I am dripping wet."

"Why, Miss Auden, so am I!"

She could no longer withstand the mischievous look in his eye and involuntarily her lips twitched into a smile, which she quickly repressed. She took his proffered arm and said as stiffly as she could manage, "In such circumstances there is no reason why I should not—in order to please my aunt, of course.

Chapter Ten

The chill, inflammation of the lungs, dropsy and the several other dreaded complaints that Phoebe Carnforth predicted, did not after all strike down her niece. However, Sara, who was unaccustomed to such a fuss being made on her behalf, found that she was enjoying herself hugely. She remained in bed for the rest of that day and for the whole of the next. During this sojourn her mind was unusually idle, enough to enable her to dwell on her frightening experience, and time and time again she did so.

It was undoubtedly Melford who had saved her life, yet she was unable to rid herself of the notion that at one point his intentions had been quite different. It would have been an easy matter for him to hold her head beneath the water sufficiently long enough to ensure her demise, thus eliminating the one threat to his anonymity. A man as ruthless as the Earl of Melford would not let pass such an opportunity of ridding himself of a bar not only to his continued safety, but to Angelina if that was where his hopes lay. It was an odd coincidence that she had almost drowned only days after Melford had, himself, pointed out the danger of the lake. But perhaps the presence of spectators nearby on the bank had made him prudent, or perhaps, as she desperately hoped, it was really her terror of drowning that had distorted his intentions.

Sara felt she would never know the whole truth, know how tempted he had been at that opportune moment to make an end of her. At this thought a sharp pain twisted around her heart, causing her to moan so loudly on one occasion that Aunt Phoebe, who had been sitting by the bed knitting, shot to her feet crying, "I must call Doctor Balfour immediately."

"It is only a bruise, Aunt Phoebe. Only a bruise."

The widow subsided into her chair again. "If I'd been allowed my way Doctor Balfour would have been called in yesterday. Immersion in cold water is no small matter. More people die of its attendant ills than of drowning."

"I did not wish Doctor Balfour to be called in; there is no reason why he should be. If I were ill it would be another matter entirely. You know very well that I cannot abide fussing."

The widow drew a sigh and continued with her knitting while Sara sank back into the pillows; the only illness from which she was suffering was a common ailment of the heart.

Whatever Melford had intended out there in the middle of the lake would remain forever entrenched in his heart. Sara did not fear for her future safety; an opportunity would not easily present itself again and she knew enough of the man she loved to appreciate that he was not a hot-head. He would not deliberately, she was sure, seek to harm her.

Early in the morning after her near fatal accident Margaret called in. "Well, you do look better!" she exclaimed. "What a sorry mess you looked yesterday."

Sara responded, as always, to her sister's cheerfulness. "I am glad, then, that I couldn't see myself. Are you going out, Meg? You're very smartly dressed for the time of day. That pelisse suits you, but shan't you be very warm in it?"

"John insists that I should be protected from the wind," she answered with a gurgle of laughter. "Isn't it hilarious? I tell you, Sara, I shall be sorry when this child is born. I'm becoming quite spoiled with all the petting I'm receiving on account of it." Her laughter died suddenly. "We're leaving here in a few minutes, Sara, so perhaps I won't be back until after my confinement."

"Must you go so soon?"

"My husband wishes to remove me, Wilhemina and his future heir from harm's way, although he will only admit to have some urgent business at Grenford on the morrow."

"All right, love, I shall ride over as soon as our guests have gone, which cannot be long now."

Margaret went to the door. "I also think it will

not be long." She opened the door a crack. "John and I will forever be in your debt, Sara. You saved our daughter's life."

"Oh, stuff and nonsense," Sara answered, and a moment later Margaret was gone, leaving her sister to wonder if anyone was troubling to chaperone Angelina whilst she, herself, was languishing under false pretences. If Sara knew her aunt the widow would be too busy fussing after the servants to worry that her youngest niece was keeping company with a rake and a highwayman. On her sister's behalf Sara didn't know which was worse.

Later in the afternoon Angelina peeped her head round the door. Sara drooped on to the pillows with more languor than she really felt, although her aunt's insistence on a closed window on such a warm day had tended to drain Sara's energy to a considerable extent.

"Are you awake?" Angelina asked in a timid voice, coming into the room as if entering the sanctum of the very sick.

"I've been awake for hours. I'm happy you've found the time to visit me."

Jealousy, apprehension and a dozen attendant emotions had made Sara sound more peevish than she normally was.

Angelina was wearing the chintz gown that Sara had to admit became her sister very well. Far better than it had suited her. The girl sat down, sulking slightly as she tended to do when scolded.

"Aunt Phoebe said I was not to worry you."

"I shall be far more worried lying here not knowing what is going on."

Angelina smiled broadly. "Oh, I can keep you informed, love." The smile faded. "I nearly died when I saw you in the water yesterday, Sara. I fancy *you* would have done if had it not been for Melford. You can't *imagine* how magnificent he was when he hauled you out."

"I'm sure he was," Sara murmured and, then, looking at her sister; "Did you enjoy your ride? You were gone, I recall, a considerable time."

Angelina's face twisted into a wry grin. "No, I did not enjoy it. It was intended that Melford would teach me how to handle a team, but he became out of patience with me before I had half a chance to master the art. You know I am not good with horses, Sara. I did warn him of it before we set off, but he would insist so that I must be good at anything I do. He really is the most irritable of men, Sara, and I had no idea of it until yesterday. Still, he *did* rescue you, which commends him to me as nothing else could."

Sara stared at her sister, at first unable to comprehend that Angelina was actually disillusioned by the earl. Then she threw back her head and laughed, imagining Melford's growing impatience when Angelina mishandled his precious horses.

"I am glad he has retained one redeeming feature," she said at last.

"You may well laugh, but you have never tried to handle a phaeton and four exceedingly peevish animals."

"I certainly have. Some years ago I drove Farley's phaeton and he was very pleased with the way I handled the ribbons."

"Farley's cattle cannot be as bad tempered as Melford's. By the by, I must tell you that Farley and Lieutenant Matthews are leaving for London tomorrow. They intend to set out for Brighton at the weekend." She sighed. "I wish I were going too. I should dearly love to see the Marine Palace and ride along the Steyne."

She sighed again and her sister said in a rallying tone, "Next year you will and as the rage of the ton too." She asked a moment later, "Is Melford going too?"

"I fully expect so. The house will be so quiet, it will be past all bearing. I'm persuaded I shall be bored to death for the rest of the summer."

Sara sat up, her heart lighter than it had been for weeks. "We must ensure that such an occurrence never happens. The weeks will fly by. We will be so busy furnishing your wardrobe, choosing materials for all the gowns you will need in London. There will be shopping expeditions to while away the time too, with bonnets, reticules, gloves, stockings and shoes to buy. Oh, all manner of things, Angelina! You won't be bored for an instant."

Angelina's face was at once transformed by

smiles and her eyes were bright. "I do believe you're right, Sara. We must begin the moment you are up."

Early the following morning Sara was awakened by the noise of carriage wheels on the driveway below her window. Farley had called in later on the previous evening to bid her goodbye and to convey the good wishes of both Lieutenant Matthews and the Earl of Melford. Typical of most young men he tarried only long enough to enquire as to her health and then quickly departed to do whatever business that was pressing him.

As the sound of wheels faded in her ears Sara rose from her bed and quickly dressed. Luckily she saw only servants as she made her way downstairs and out into the gardens. She walked for a while, revelling in the heavily scented air of the cool morning. The house was hers again, her heart would mend. Melford was gone, but the pain of that knowledge overcame her relief.

She knew he would not return. There would be no call for him to do so as it would be many months before Farley paid another visit to his country home. Indeed, with Angelina and Aunt Phoebe in London, there would be no need of it as Papa would, no doubt, join them for long periods. Sara would resist all invitations for herself. She would remain here at Beechleys, nursing the pain within her heart until it faded into nothing more than a memory.

Sara seated herself in her favourite spot and after a moment or two the birds dared to approach her. For once she did not heed them. Her future spread before her and every prospect of it was uninviting. She did not want to be merely a maiden aunt to her brothers' and sisters' children, and a reliable help in times of illness, but it appeared now that there was nothing else for her to do. The only alternative was to marry Charles Hanley and that, to Sara now, was impossible.

The affection of her family was something she would always possess, but even they would not be able to shield her from the fear that, despite Farley's pledge that his foolhardy involvement had occurred only once, Melford might persuade him into further daring schemes. Nor would it ease her grief if the earl were to become careless and allow himself to be caught; and for highway robbery there was only one punishment.

Whilst her sister was indulging in morbid thoughts Angelina was just emerging from her bedchamber. She hesitated before coming down the stairs, for just then she overheard someone entering the hall.

"You'll be anxious to be off then, Melford," Sir Henry was saying. "Glad to have had you here though. About time m'son brought some real bloods into the house. Never did like the dandy set he was associated with a time back."

"I'm obliged to you, sir, and for your hospitality," replied the other. "I wonder if it would be convenient for me to discuss with you a personal matter before I go. It's a family matter, one that concerns your daughter."

Sir Henry eyed him in astonishment, and smoothing his chintz morning coat in an absent way, said, "Why, certainly, Melford. Come this way, into the library. We won't be disturbed in there and I have some excellent sherry I'd like you to try. I'd be obliged for your opinion on it."

Angelina in her hidden position clapped one hand over her mouth to stifle a gasp, her eyes wide with wonder. As the library door closed she turned and ran in a most unladylike way to her aunt's room.

Mrs. Carnforth, still in deshabille, her nightcap askew her grey locks, was taken aback at the sight of her wild-eyed niece abroad at so early an hour. She replaced her cup of chocolate on the tray and, closing her eyes, she pressed one hand to her breast. "Pray, do not tell me, Angelina. I know it already. Sara has contracted inflammation of the lungs just as I predicted."

• "As far as I know," said the astonished girl, "Sara is as hale and hearty as always. It will take more than a dip in the lake to finish her off."

"Then it's your father. Henry has had a seizure. Do not try to spare me."

Angelina skipped across to the four-poster and drew the curtains fully. "No, Papa is well. I saw him but a few moments ago, although he may well have a seizure at any time. Melford has asked to speak to him on 'a family matter', one that concerns his daughter!"

Aunt Phoebe gaped. "I don't believe it."

"I heard it with my own ears, Aunt. There can be only one matter he wishes to discuss with Papa."

"Indeed. *Indeed.*" Aunt Phoebe's eyes grew large at the anticipation of it. A moment later she was inspecting Angelina critically. "You must change your gown and comb your hair. You'd better run along now."

Angelina laughed. "I look perfectly respectable, Aunt Phoebe. Besides, I have no intention of accepting him."

"Of course you are to refuse him. It is always prudent to refuse once."

"You don't understand, Aunt Phoebe. I have no intention of accepting him at all. At least I don't think so." She examined herself airily in the cheval mirror. "I expect I shall have lots of suitors once I've made my debut, and it won't do my reputation one jot of harm for the Earl of Melford to have offered for me first. Oh, I do declare it is so exciting!"

Mrs. Carnforth stared at her niece for a moment or two, during which, it seemed, she was speechless.

"Why you brass-faced chit," she gasped at last. "You mean to make an end of me." She flung back the bed-covers. "Ring for Betsy. I must rise immediately whilst I can still summon up the strength."

"Aunt Phoebe," Angelina said in a soothing tone, "Only *think*. My refusal will not daunt a man of Lord Melford's stature. He is the type of man only to be encouraged by a refusal. When we are in London he will be my constant escort, which, in turn, will ensure my social success."

Phoebe Carnforth drew a robe around her ample figure. "I think, Angelina, you *are* going to be the end of me. I don't envy your husband when you choose him, really I don't."

Some time later Angelina and her aunt emerged from the bedchamber anxious to hide their air of excitement. Phoebe Carnforth was well aware of the stir her niece would make in fashionable circles once it was known that a personage no less than the Earl of Melford had made an offer for her *before* the Season had even begun.

The two were in time to see Sir Henry and the earl solemnly shaking hands at the door. When the earl had gone and the butler withdrawing the two ladies hurried down the stairs to Sir Henry who had the air of a man in a stupor.

"Well, Henry," his sister bade, "tell us."

"Do tell us, Papa," urged his daughter.

"Told him she was too young. Hadn't had a Season yet. Better wait a while I told him."

"Yes, yes, that was to be expected. He'd expect you to say that, Henry. Do go on."

He stared belligerently at his sister. "I'm trying to, aren't I? He said I'd mistaken his intentions. Wanted to offer for Sara."

Angelina gasped. "Oh, no! He wouldn't. Why, he's hardly spoken to Sara! He's been fixing his interest with *me*!"

Her aunt turned to her. "Silence, girl, or you'll go back to your room until you learn to guard your tongue." Then she turned eagerly to her brother again. "This goes beyond all I'd hoped. Pray continue, Henry."

"Was bound to tell him m'sister believed Sara had an . . . er . . . fondness for him and it seemed to please the fellow. Grand chap, Melford. Make a grand son-in-law. Mind you, I don't fancy that chit as Sara's mother-in-law."

"Ariadne Merrick is no longer a chit, Henry. She'll be fifty, I'll be bound. Anyway if she were a two headed dragon it wouldn't signify. Did Melford say anything else?"

"Said plenty. He waved away my praises of Sara. He said I needn't tell him—he knew. Then he went on to explain what *he* could offer *her*. I tell you, Phoebe, I'd never felt so queer in all my life, not even after I'd offered for Fanny. Gave him my blessing, needless to say."

The widow began to chuckle and Angelina at the

sight of her relatives' satisfaction stamped her foot. "It's only because he feels sorry for her."

"Do you really believe so?" Aunt Phoebe asked in mock surprise. "This is the second offer in a week, you know."

Angelina stared at her aunt. "Second?" she asked.

"Charles Hanley made an offer only the other day."

Angelina looked vexed again. "Charles Hanley doesn't count. If everyone sang my praises instead of Sara's this might well be *my* second offer!" She turned on her heel and swept into the drawing room, rudely pushing aside a maid who had unwisely got into her way. As the door slammed shut Phoebe Carnforth began to chuckle again.

She caught at her brother's arm. "Come along, Henry. I think we both deserve a glass of madeira. Angelina will soon recover her good humour and be glad for her sister."

"D'you realize, Phoebe," he said in a shocked voice, "that all my children will soon be married? Farley has about him the look of a man moonstruck, and I don't suppose Angelina will tarry far behind once she's launched into Society."

"What a pleasant matter to contemplate. We shall be kept busy just keeping count of all the babies as they come along."

Sir Henry shook his head, refusing to be cheered.

"We're getting old, Phoebe. Old. Never realized it until today."

"Yes, dear, we're getting old, and thank goodness we no longer have the problems of the very young. That's a blessing in itself.

"A glass of madeira always revives you, Henry. Come along now. Don't dally any longer in this draughty hall. It's bad for your rheumatism."

In the garden Sara had lost track of time; she was only aware that she had a great deal of it to while away. When she heard footsteps heralding the approach of an intruder into her thoughts, she got to her feet as she did not wish to be found idle.

"Lord Melford," she said, her confusion the greater for having thought him gone.

"I am relieved to find you well recovered from your ordeal, Miss Auden."

"Yes, I am completely recovered," she answered, keeping her eyes downcast, "and although I remember little of what happened I am told it is to you that I owe my life. I thank you for it."

"May I sit with you?"

She hesitated for a moment before she nodded and after handing her to the seat he sat down beside her. "I was happy to be of service to you then, Miss Auden, as always."

Sara's hands were clasped demurely in front of her, her eyes still downcast, and it was impossible for anyone to guess her delight the sight of him had created. "You are too kind," she murmured. His mood was odd, she thought; it held nothing of the mockery she had come to expect or the menace she had sometimes seen.

"Miss Auden, I have something to ask you . . ." She looked at him then. His eyes held hers. He hesitated but a moment before asking, "Will you marry me?"

She stared at him incredulously. "Marry you?" She looked away, her mind working frantically. "This is most unexpected."

"I felt that nothing could be gained by waiting further. I have engagements which might prevent us from meeting for months. To be honest, Sara, I see no advantage in a delay for us."

"I understand that." Hard on the heels of her initial shock at a second proposal in a matter of days came a terrible vision; a honeymoon in some isolated spot, a dreadful accident, and a broken-hearted bridegroom returning home, safe and free to Melford Park.

"I beg you, Lord Melford . . ."

"Richard."

She raised her eyes to his. "I beg you to tell me why you wish to marry me."

His eyes betrayed a little surprise and then he smiled, lifting her hand to his lips. "Can't you guess?"

The mockery was there again. Her less-than-steady hand was withdrawn as she answered in no more than a whisper, "Yes, I believe I can."

"And your answer? I must tell you, your father has been good enough to give his blessing, so have no worry on that score."

She laughed, a laugh with a bitter edge to it. "No doubt he does, but *you* must know I cannot accept. Surely you didn't expect me to?"

She felt, rather than saw, him stiffen. "Sara, don't let the circumstances of our meeting affect your decision. No one apart from our two selves need ever know of it."

Her smile was a tight one. "That is sufficient, Lord Melford. Pray speak of it no more. My decision is made."

"Your pride is excessive, Miss Auden."

His voice was cold and she longed to hear it infused with warmth again. "It is not a matter of pride, Lord Melford, but of decency. You must think me a simpleton were I to accept such a proposal."

He got to his feet, drawing himself up to full height. "Sara, this foolishness has gone on long enough. You have, I assure you, made your point and and I am suitably humbled, but I cannot regret our meeting whatever way it came about." Obtusely she kept her eyes downcast and a moment later he said, "Should you change your mind I shall be at Melford Park during the coming week and after that at my home at Brighton. Are you accompanying your sister and aunt to London later this year?"

"No, I'm staying here."

"So it is unlikely that we shall meet unless you choose that we do so."

"I shall not."

"Sara, Sara!" he said in a low and urgent voice. "You are impossible. Do you wish to remain here the rest of your days while other women are fulfilled?"

"You go beyond what is proper, my lord."

"Very well. It is obvious that I make no impression on your emotions, except to fill you with a loathing I do not believe I deserve. I will say no more, except to wish you well and happy when you sit on the shelf with nothing but your pride to keep you company."

She jumped to her feet and brushed past him, stifling her sobs with her hand. As she emerged from the shrubbery she cannoned into no other personage than Aunt Phoebe—the last person Sara would have chosen to meet at that particular time.

"Sara, my dear girl, what has alarmed you into this state. Fancy wandering out at this time of the day, straight from your bed with no parasol or shawl to protect you. How foolhardy you are. You must go to your room immediately and tidy yourself; I must tell you Melford has . . ."

"I've just seen him," Sara gasped, "and I must

tell you, Aunt Phoebe, before you say anything more, I have refused him."

The parasol Mrs. Carnforth had been gaily twirling when she encountered her niece now clattered to the path. "Refused him! Refused him! I don't believe it's possible. Even a blind mind could see that you're in love with the man."

"Please, Aunt Phoebe, I can't explain. I just cannot marry Melford, and that's final."

Phoebe Carnforth closed her eyes and swayed precariously on her feet. Fearful of her swooning and perhaps injuring herself on the path Sara caught her arm and began to lead her bemused aunt towards the house just as Melford, himself, emerged from the shrubbery. The widow moaned again at the sight of him and Sara tightened her grip on her arm.

Melford glanced from one lady to the other. "Is something amiss? Has Mrs. Carnforth taken ill?"

"Yes, and it's all your fault!" cried Sara. "Why did you ever have to come here to plague us!"

She turned her back on him and helped her swooning aunt into the house. "You must go to your bed, Aunt Phoebe," Sara told her. "I will bring a glass of hartshorn and water to your room immediately. I feel that should be sufficient to revive you. There will be no need to burn feathers."

The widow put one hand out to stay her niece. "Send Betsy. I cannot bear to have you near me just now. I could understand your refusing Charles

Hanley but to refuse Melford . . ." Words failed her and she merely shook her head as she hauled herself up the stairs by way of the baluster rail.

Sara watched her go, although tears blurred her vision long before Aunt Phoebe had reached the top. Angelina, who was just coming out of the small drawing room, stopped in her tracks when she saw her sister in the hall. She tossed back her head in a defiant gesture, hissed "Traitor," and marched to the stairs with her head averted.

While she was still trying to think of something soothing to say to her sister Sara whirled round on hearing a noise behind her. Emerging red-faced from her father's library was none other than Charles Hanley. He shot her a vexed look, half-bowed and, retrieving his hat and gloves from the butler, marched erectly through the front door that Maitland was holding open. The butler's face was as inscrutable as ever despite having witnessed some odd scenes since Miss Sara had arrived with her aunt.

Sara put one hand to her reeling head. "Papa, what did Mr. Hanley want with you?" she asked although she already suspected the answer.

Sir Henry drew himself up indignantly as the butler closed the door again. "The puppy had the impudence to beseech me to press you to accept his suit. Told me you'd refused him once but he wouldn't accept it as final. Told him you'd had a better offer, and even if you hadn't I wouldn't press you against your wishes. Insolence. Never did like Denvoe's clan. Too puffed up by their own consequence."

"Dearest, Papa."

His scowl disappeared and he smiled down at her. "Two offers, hmm? You don't have to marry that coxcombe, do you, puss? Was that Phoebe I saw going upstairs? For a moment it looked as if she was having an attack of the vapours. Thought she'd have more sense at her age. Can't abide vapourish females and never could. It's all been too much for her I dare say."

Sara's own smile faded. "She may well be having an attack of some kind. You see, I have refused Melford, Papa, so don't you be cross with me too."

He put his arm around her shoulders. "Not interested in wedlock, eh? Pity. Grand fellow. Excellent stud, y'know."

"Papa!"

He laughed gruffly. "Cattle, m'dear; over at Melford Park. Shan't quiz you, Sara. It's your life. Like I told Hanley; Don't come to me, I said. Sara's word on the matter is good enough for me—and any gentleman if it comes to that. He didn't like that, but I didn't care. It might have been a different matter if he'd come to me first as he ought. Spineless jackass."

She laid her head on his shoulder. For a moment she was tempted to confide in her father and tell him exactly why she had been forced to refuse

Richard Merrick's offer of marriage while longing to throw herself into his arms in a way that would cause Aunt Phoebe to faint away completely. But if she attempted to persuade her prosaic father that the fourth Earl of Melford was also the most elusive highwayman in the country he would be bound to have her confined to an asylum forthwith. Sara wasn't at all sure that she wouldn't soon be in Bedlam anyway. At that moment her father was the only person in the house, apart from the servants who didn't count, who had no cause to feel animosity towards her, and to be on bad terms with both Angelina and Aunt Phoebe would soon turn her brain to be sure.

Suddenly the tears she had been holding back began to flow down her cheeks.

"There, there," her father crooned; awkwardly patting her arm, "no need to take on so. You don't have to wed anyone if you don't want to. No one will cast you out, never fear. Why, if you feel like this about it I'll withdraw my permission! That should settle it quite nicely."

At such a monumental, yet endearing, misunderstanding on her behalf she again laid her head on his shoulder. "Oh, Papa," she said in a muffled voice and, burying her head in her startled parent's shoulder, she sobbed until she thought her heart would break.

Chapter Eleven

Sara found that she was spending most of her time during the ensuing days avoiding both her sister and her aunt. Angelina, pointedly, sulked despite Sara's initial attempt to humour her and although Aunt Phoebe did not cut Sara completely her manner was decidedly frosty. So, as Sir Henry went about his business and had neither the time nor the inclination to coddle his eldest daughter in her time of need, Sara went about hers. She set about jobs that had needed attending to for some time and many that did not need doing, sparing herself not a jot in the process. The servants of Beechleys were so impressed by their mistress's ardour that they were only too eager to go about the tasks she set them. For Sara it all helped to keep her mind occupied and prevent her from dwelling upon her own unhappiness. In the words of a novel that she had read during her stay in Harrogate she reckoned she had been allowed to reach the gates of Paradise only to be turned away.

Some five days after the Earl of Melford had left Beechleys the atmosphere, except at mealtimes which Sir Henry invariably attended, was still decidedly chill. Sara knew her aunt and Angelina were ensconced in the small drawing room with all the latest fashion magazines, going about the important business of choosing a suitable wardrobe for Angelina. Being forewarned, the small drawing room was the one place Sara made a point to avoid, especially as the sight of her sister deciding upon styles and materials for gowns, the number of stockings and petticoats she would need, and so on, painfully reminded her that if Fate had been kind she, herself, might have been choosing her trousseau at this same time.

But Sara could not help but be curious when from the upper landing she espied Maitland taking in a tea tray at an unaccustomed hour. She hurried down the stairs crying, "Maitland, wait!" as the butler emerged from the room a moment later.

The butler waited as he was bid. "Yes, Miss Sara. Did you wish for something?"

"Has a visitor arrived, Maitland?"

"Mr. Plant, Miss Sara."

She felt both relief and disappointment. It was foolish as she knew; Melford would not return, nor would she want him to.

Her smile was faint. "Very well, Maitland. You may go along. I shall see myself in."

Sara quickly tidied her hair and smoothed her gown before going over to the drawing room, but she hesitated to open the door fully when she heard her aunt's shrill voice.

"I tell you, John, that girl hasn't been the same since we had that encounter with that rascally highwayman. Oh, she kept her calm at the time, but it's my belief that it affected her nerves, and who is to wonder? I was shockingly unnerved myself. Why, she even thought that Melford was Bill Kersey when she first set eyes on him. Depend upon it, John, that is why she refused him. It's all to do with the highwayman! She's behaved very oddly since then. She was always the most even tempered soul before that."

Having heard enough Sara pushed open the doors fully in time to hear her brother-in-law reply, "I am grieved to hear you say so, Aunt Phoebe. Both Meg and myself have always had a great deal of regard for Sara. I dare say she'll be glad to know that the scoundrel has been apprehended at last, and by now should be safely in jail."

The cosy domestic scene, her aunt with tea kettle poised, swam before Sara's eyes. She rushed into the room, not caring if her aunt did believe her unhinged and had her removed to Bedlam.

"How do you know, John?" she demanded.

Her worthy brother-in-law shot to his feet. "Hello, Sara. I was hoping to see you. Good news, isn't it? Knew you'd be glad."

"It cannot be true!"

John Plant smiled happily. "The news is not general yet, but I have it from a first hand witness. I met the gentleman at the smithy at Grenford. He'd spent the night, two nights ago, at the White Duck at Stamford. The rogue was apprehended there by two Bow Street Runners who had been on his trail for days. It seems that he held up the York Stage the day before. All this time he'd been a regular visitor to the inn—and a popular one too. The gentleman I spoke to had actually supped ale with the villain. Said he would have sworn he was a gentleman of the first style, which just goes to prove that one never can tell."

Sara twisted her hands in anguish. Her thoughts immediately flew to Farley, even though he had promised he had been involved on only one occasion; one occasion was enough to hang him. She looked anxiously at her brother-in-law. "Was there anyone with him at the time?" John stared at his boots. "Was there anyone with him, John?" she insisted, aware that her voice was rising.

John glanced apologetically at Aunt Phoebe and Angelina, saying in a low voice that could only just be heard, "The landlord's daughter."

Aunt Phoebe's gasp echoed around the room. "Excuse me," Sara murmured. "I need some air," and without further hesitation rushed across the room and out on to the balcony beyond.

"You see how strangely she behaves," the widow complained. "I tell you it has affected her mind."

Meanwhile Sara was pacing up and down the

balcony, her mind in a tumult of agony. A million jumbled thoughts passed through her tortured brains in the space of minutes, even hastily contrived and foolish plans to rescue him from his jailers.

Inevitably she came to blame herself. It suddenly occurred to her that she had been too foolish in fearing for herself; she should have married him and, perhaps, if she had given him an heir he would have given up his thieving, libertine ways and become more responsible.

"It's all my fault," she cried aloud.

The ways of a highwayman must seem adventurous to a man like Melford who was most probably bored with the ways of Polite Society.

The sound of a carriage on the driveway startled her out of her thoughts. She hesitated a moment. She was in no mood to receive visitors, who, since the rout, had called on them frequently. Lifting her skirts she fled into the shrubbery.

It was here that the object of all her anguish found her, pacing nervously near the seat on which he had made his proposal. Her agitation was so great that she didn't hear his approach.

"Sara!" he said sharply. "I've been searching the gardens for you."

She whirled round at the sound of his voice. For one incredulous moment she stared at him before sinking to the ground in a dead faint for the first time in her life. When she regained her senses she was reclining on the garden seat with two strong arms firmly supporting her.

"My love, what is it?" she heard him say. "Are you ill, or is my presence so obnoxious to you? Only say so and I will go, for good this time."

"Oh, why are you here?" she managed to gasp. "I didn't think to see you again."

The anxious look in his eyes vanished to be replaced by a gleam of amusement. "Are you so pleased to be found wrong, Sara? Is that why you swooned?"

"Yes, Richard. Yes."

He drew her close. Sara decided that her mind was still befuddled by his sudden appearance and that was why she allowed him to kiss her in such a breathless way.

When he released her his expression was a triumphant one. "Sir Henry was not wrong when he spoke of your feelings for me. I knew you could not be indifferent however much you denied it."

She put her hand to his lips. "I never was indifferent to you, Richard. But why do you come?"

"For this. Precisely this. I had to come to try and persuade you to marry me before I went away."

"Foolish, foolish man. Don't you know it's dangerous? Who knows of your presence here?"

He sat back a little, although his arms were still tightly about her. "Many people. The servants of course. Your aunt herself directed me to the gardens."

Sara closed her eyes. "Imprudent love! How did you escape?"

"Escape? It was simple. When I told Mrs. Carnforth without delay that I had come to make one last appeal to you she told me you were to be found out here."

"How can you jest at a time like this? I'm talking about your escape from jail. For all we know they may have pursued you here." She sat up straight. "They may be here now. Give me but five minutes to fill a cloak bag and we shall leave for Folkestone immediately. We can be in France within two days if we hurry."

He pressed one hand to her forehead. "I fear you have had too much of the sun, my love. I have never been pursued by jailers in my life, for the simple reason that I have never been in jail. All my bills and obligations are met promptly. My father was a prudent man in affairs of money and he taught his children well."

"Don't tease me, Richard. You know full well what I am speaking of."

"I assure you I don't. I have never been in jail I promise you. I should hate it. Such filthy places, I am told, with no valeting facilities whatsoever."

"Oh, how can you jest so?" She brushed away his hand. "Whom did they arrest if it wasn't you?"

"I'm sure I don't know. Whom do you think they arrested?"

She looked at him searchingly. "Were you at the White Duck at Stamford the night before last?"

"I wouldn't dream of being seen in that den of iniquity. I was at Melford Park eating a solitary dinner and reflecting on the iniquities of love, much to my man's disgust. Who has been spreading filthy tales of me?"

Sara beamed. "Then it wasn't you the Runners arrested."

"Haven't I been telling you that? Now, my love, what is this all about?"

Sara frowned. "I still can't understand who they arrested if it wasn't you."

Melford was frowning too. Suddenly enlightenment came. "Bill Kersey was arrested two days ago. The news is spreading fast. The trial promises to be most interesting, especially if they call as witness those poor girls he had abducted during his career on the High Toby." He looked at her in amazement. "Why, love, you couldn't have believed it was I?"

Sara's lips drew into a thin line. "Why did you pretend to be him, Richard? Did you do it for a wager?"

"You are ill, dearest. We must send for a physician immediately." He attempted to help her to her feet. "Mrs. Carnforth is best qualified to attend you, not I."

"Please, Richard, I wish to remain here for a moment or two longer." He sat down again although his face still wore the worried frown. "Richard, have you ever been, or pretended to be, a highwayman?"

"Certainly not. I'm not a schoolboy. I outgrew such pranks with my schooldays."

Sara felt faint again but his presence sustained her to a small degree. "I've made such a dreadful mistake," she murmured. "He looked so very much like you."

"You can't mean to tell me you thought I was this scoundrel, this robber, this abductor of innocent women." His voice was angry and she feared him again; she feared she had lost what she had only just found. Then suddenly he let out a loud shout of laughter, causing great flights of birds to rise up from the trees. "Is this what all your indignation and rage has been about?"

"What else?" she answered, fighting back her tears.

"You couldn't have had a good look at him, Sara. Surely he was masked."

"Yes, indeed, and mufflered, but his hair was clean and curled like yours, and his eyes . . . his expression." She blushed. "Oh, I cannot explain."

"I'm relieved that the Runners require rather more evidence than the expression in a man's eyes before making an arrest or I might be on my way to the scaffold today."

She clapped her hands over her ears. "Oh, do not speak of it! I cannot bear to think of it any more!"

He drew her close and his lips were close to hers. "Did it distress you very much?"

She put her arms around his neck. "You cannot imagine the pain it caused me, my dearest. I have been so foolish and I'm ashamed. Will you forgive me?"

"Forgiving you has never been in question. My greatest problem was in finding a way to persuade you to trust and love me."

"But I do."

He smiled at her. "So much so that you were prepared to abandon your scruples and desert your family to come with me to safety."

She rested her head on his shoulder. "I realized the moment I saw you again that whatever you were I could not live without you."

"Then you will marry me?"

"Oh, yes."

Moments later she was extricating herself from his tight embrace. "But you admitted it. You warned me not to speak of it to Farley." He drew away, his expression sheepish. "I mean to know, Richard, so you will be so good as to explain why you allowed me to believe you were the highwayman."

His eyes opened wide. "I did not, believe me. I had no idea that you believed me to be a common highwayman. My noble ancestors will be rattling their bones at such an outrageous suggestion."

"But you believed me to be aware of *something,*

Richard. I know you are not one of Farley's usual cronies, so what is it that involves Farley? When you warned me not to mention it to my brother I was quite terrified."

He took her hand and raised it to his lips. "Poor love, I have caused you much anguish, but I promise to give you nothing but happiness in the future."

"You speak very prettily. I cannot help but feel that you are well-practised in the art."

"Would you rather me behave and speak like a bungling clodpole?"

She recalled Charles Hanley and his offer of marriage. She smiled to herself and shook her head. Withdrawing her hand she murmured demurely, "Your explanation, please."

Melford drew a sigh and, holding her steady gaze, said, "It is nothing that needs concern you, Sara, of that you may be sure."

"My family's affairs have always concerned me. I cannot be happy for my own sake until my mind is relieved of this last anxiety."

"You have already promised to be my wife. I have no intention of releasing you from your pledge."

Her face relaxed into a smile again. "Nor will I wish to be released, my lord."

"I like it much better when you call me Richard."

She was serious again. "Richard, I don't for a

moment believe it's serious, but do tell me, I beg you."

He gave her a small smile. "You are a persistent woman and I foresee all manner of problems arising in the future. However, seeing you insist, I shall tell you, but you won't like it."

"I didn't imagine that I would," she answered dryly.

"I did try to explain the day we were both by the lake, when you asked how the scheme was embarked upon, but as you were thinking of something quite different at the time I dare say I shall have to be more explicit now."

Sara composed herself. She was half-afraid, admittedly, but nothing seemed important now that her future was settled in such a delightful way. She stole a look at him from beneath her lashes. "Pray continue, Richard."

He seemed to draw a deep breath and for one who usually spoke with such deliberation and sureness it was odd for him to be so hesitant of speech.

"Some days before we came down here I was at Brooks's. Quite by accident I overheard a conversation between Lieutenant Matthews and your brother." He was speaking quickly now as if he wanted it to be done with, as indeed he did.

"It appears that your brother wishes to marry, yet he is sensible enough to appreciate that a new mistress here in the foreseeable future would put you into some kind of wilderness." Sara gave a little gasp and he went on quickly. "So it was suggested that a few eligible young men were invited to accompany him down here." Sara felt her cheeks redden, but she kept her eyes on her hands which were clasped about her knees. "To give your brother credit he doubted the wisdom of such a plan as soon as it was mentioned, but he felt that nothing could be lost by trying it out. My name was one of those suggested—the most likely candidate in fact."

He went on even more quickly when it appeared that Sara was about to say something. "Your brother and his friend were totally unaware that I had overheard the discussion of their crack-brained scheme. In truth, Sara, at the time I was bored with the London scene and anxious to escape an entanglement which was proving embarrassing." At her sharp look he hastily added, "Oh, it is quite finished; even before I met you, my love.

"When I made a point of seeking out your brother late in the evening I made it easy for him to invite me. In fact I made it difficult for him not to." He hesitated a moment. "I wanted to see this rustic spinster who was causing her brother to usher the most unlikely young men into her company. How was I to know she would in fact be a beauty and that I would fall in love with her on sight?"

When she raised her eyes to meet his they were soft and shining, although his were anxious and more than a little afraid. And then quite unexpectedly she started to laugh.

"So that's what it was all about. Dear Mr. Cheviot, Mr. Booker and Desmond Adams. If only I had known." Her eyes grew wide. "Surely not Lieutenant Matthews also?"

"I believe he was here just to lend your brother support. It is befitting that in doing so he has also been caught in the love trap himself. He is quite moonstruck over your sister and will not be far from her side during her stay in the capital."

Sara began to laugh even more. "Oh, heavens, I wish I had known! How amusing it would have been."

"You are not angry, my love?" asked the earl, who was hardly daring to believe his luck.

"Angry, Richard? It is the most amusing scheme I have ever heard. Dear Farley. I never knew he cared so much. I'm quite touched. And I was so much on my dignity with you, Richard. You must have considered me an undoubted prude."

"No, no, darling Sara. When you told me you knew why I was here, I understood your mortification, only it was rather irritating later on when you would have nothing of me even though I was in earnest."

Sara went off into peals of laughter again and as she searched for a handkerchief the earl withdrew his and gently dabbed at her tears. "His face, Richard," she gasped. "You should have seen his face when I told him I knew what he'd done. Poor Farley! I dare say he'll leave others to their own love life in future and attend to his own."

Melford drew her into his arms again. "You can't know how relieved I am that you're amused and not angry."

Serious now, she answered, "And you cannot know how relieved I am that you're not a highwayman, which is far more important," adding in a tone of censure, "Having fallen for me on sight, as you declare, I feel that you did seek out Angelina's company rather more than was necessary. You raised the poor girl's hopes unnecessarily, not to mention my jealousy on that score."

"For that I am sorry," he answered in a tone that belied his words, "but I needed some reason to stay and to return, for you gave me no encouragement and, as you will no doubt agree, as I was something of a scoundrel I did not hesitate to allow everyone to believe she was the reason. Besides when you so obviously found my company so unattractive, one who did was soothing to my injured pride. Angelina is an exceedingly pretty girl . . ." He smiled as she looked at him fiercely. "I dare say that in a year or two she might almost be as beautiful as her sister."

Sara settled happily into his arms. "Papa has withdrawn his permission, you may as well be warned."

"I'm sure your father can be persuaded to change

his mind again. He is most anxious for your happiness and almost as anxious to have me as his son-in-law."

"You are too full of your own consequence," she retorted.

"That cannot be after all you have made me suffer."

After he had kissed her again she murmured happily, "This really is improper, Richard."

"Your aunt is a lady who is well aware of what is proper and I'm sure she will join us when she deems it time to do so. It was Mrs. Carnforth who directed me here, so until she does seek us out here we will stay."

Sara demurred no further. She put her face up for his kiss.

At that precise moment Farley Auden was driving his team with unnecessary fury along the Brighton Road, reflecting sourly that of all Sara had done for him he had failed miserably in the one thing he had ever tried to do for her.

Romantic Fiction

If you like novels of passion and daring adventure that take you to the very heart of human drama, these are the books for you.

☐ AFTER—Anderson	Q2279	1.50
☐ THE DANCE OF LOVE—Dodson	23110-0	1.75
☐ A GIFT OF ONYX—Kettle	23206-9	1.50
☐ TARA'S HEALING—Giles	23012-0	1.50
☐ THE TROIKA BELLE—Morris	23013-9	1.75
☐ THE DEFIANT DESIRE—Klem	13741-4	1.75
☐ LOVE'S TRIUMPHANT HEART—Ashton	13771-6	1.75
☐ MAJORCA—Dodson	13740-6	1.75